Gascoigne Mackie

Poems dramatic and democratic

Gascoigne Mackie

Poems dramatic and democratic

ISBN/EAN: 9783337304690

Printed in Europe, USA, Canada, Australia, Japan

Cover: Foto ©Andreas Hilbeck / pixelio.de

More available books at **www.hansebooks.com**

POEMS

DRAMATIC AND DEMOCRATIC

BY

GASCOIGNE MACKIE

(Author of "The Ballad of Pity," and other Poems.)

London :

ELLIOT STOCK, 62, PATERNOSTER ROW, E.C.

Clacton = on = Sea :

LINE BROTHERS, PRINTERS AND PUBLISHERS.

1893.

CONTENTS

THE NEW SPIRIT

The catalogue of common things

Is no more common, no more dull ;

Not solely in the bird that sings,

Not wholly in the Beautiful

So-called, lives wonder and the hope

Of the great future ; nay, the dawn

Of Science brings a wider scope :

Poetic imag'ry is worn

To shreds and patches, fain would seek

A deeper impulse, and renew

Lost ways of Nature ; so with meek

And steadfast eye let me review,

And trace here with a truthful hand
The landscape at my feet.

Behold--
A morning toward the close of March.
Grey clouds in sullen masses roll'd,
With patches of azure, overarch
The earth; and gusts of warm wind stir
The pregnant trees, and swell the seeds
Unseen, of Spring; while lovelier
Glimpses of sun athwart the meads
Wake song, and lend the grass a hue
Of livelier green—a hundred roods
Of vale and meadow I can view
Here from this knoll, till distant woods
Sink in the circling gray, and mist
Obscure the hills behind ;—what wealth
Of lights and shadows melt and twist,
Quiver with mirth and sport in stealth,

Linger and lengthen, quicken amain,
Play hide-and-seek with breeze and trees,
Race over the meadows and rest again
Beneath bare elms!

                  Our hopes increase
With every hour : fresh marvels wake
The heart to happiness, and send
A challenge to the soul to take
Plain facts, and use them for her end.

A mile away, a railway bank
Confronts the eye : when all is still
At twilight, and I sit and thank
The sinking sun, and drink my fill
Of quiet thought with all that is,
Lost in deep-breathing reverie,
Half waiting till an angel kiss
My lips to song : lo ! suddenly

Between the vision of my gaze,

The silence of the evening star,

'Mid drift of smoke and sunset-haze

Sweeps the leviathan afar

With thund'rous echoes, ringing rods

Of steel, and force devouring space.

O, surely men shall be as gods

Knowing the Good and Evil, place

Their feet in pride upon the globe,

Ransack the mysteries of the earth,

While Nature's splendour like a robe

Clothes this more glorious second birth :

Old things must pass, the mind expands,

Parochial beauty, selfish joys

Dilate, the general heart demands

Expression. Shall no fusing voice

Chant in plain strains the strife and stress :

Man's work for man, life leased anew,

The progress through the patientness

Of the great dead, our fathers, who

Laboured in secret for us ? Yea—

A mighty nation at my back

Pushes me forward, bids me say

(Albeit these youthful tones must lack

The classic poise) that "man ascends

From step to step by slow degrees

That cannot lapse : ample amends

Wait upon effort ; this that frees

Binds by new laws, sure laws for ever,

The relentless laws of liberty.

Man's link with Nature none can sever,

Man's mastery a fool may see."

'Tis sung aloud by storm and cloud

And cleansing cataract ;

The Race is born to Empire

That can grapple with the fact.

ENDYMION'S APPEAL

Clasp me for ever in thy silent arms,

And press thy sculptured lips close to mine own,

So shall I need no other love but thine:

For all the woods are wild with choirs of birds,

And every lake has leagues of whispering reeds,

And o'er the foam the mermaids faintly call;

E'en the vine-tendril tightens: O my love,

Mine unseen love, I am thy chosen one,

Faithful but mortal still, smit deep and sore,

For ever waiting and for ever sad:

Thou would'st not have me quit thee for a maid

Nurtured in men's abodes, e'en though her form

Proudly should move, with all love's argosy

Impearled, or lightly spread her laughing sails

To the passionate gusts of Spring — Lend me thy
  strength

To walk immortal on these heights alone ;

With thee my soul can scorn the ills of life,

Without thee, I am as the sliding stream

That purls a wayward course mid flower and fern

Down through green dingles to the deep beyond :—

The lowliest find love's equal and a home,

The dead are with the dead, companions all

In bliss or sorrow : only I perforce

Am ravished with impossible love of thee,

Striving to reach up with my wingless arms :

O awful goddess, whose cloud-sandal'd feet

Have paced a thousand centuries away,

Watching this earth wheel fiercely on and on

Through death and change revolving ; dost thou stoop

To stab with beauty an ephemeral youth,

Whose voice but deepened, when thy mysteries

Bade hush his saucy notes ? — no skylark now,

Warbling shrill dawn-songs 'neath an April sun,

But stern and resolute : nerve and sinew set

To wrestle and to race.

                    O why, white witch,

Wilt thou not let me live as other men ?

Why should I loiter on this lonesome steep,

Why bivouac under stars innumerable,

Innumerable stars and liquid chasms

Of silent peace ? whence issuing from a cloud,

Thy naked grandeur breaks upon my watch

And whirls me heaven-ward, and I know not where,

Only this ecstasy will slay me soon ;

And other shepherds, as they wind at dawn

Up the thin mountain-path, carelessly singing

Of kine and harvest-home, the pastoral life,

Will start to stumble on the form of one

Too heavily sleeping, to be called and hear.

Ah, but thou lov'st me, else I could not dare

To raise mere mortal eyes and gaze on thee;

Thou lov'dst me first; while still a careless lad,

One night in sleep the strange ambrosial musk

That marks thine advent, and all other gods,

Stole through my senses, and the world was changed.

I woke at dawn and longed to sleep again;

And when I slept, I cursed the chain of sleep

That showed but held me from thee.

But at last

Thou didst descend and fold me in thine arms;

I felt the life-beat of the universe,

Pressing mine ear against thy breast; I clung,

And let thy deity raise me from the earth,

Only by thee supported: ah! what bliss!

In thine austerity glowed deeper fires

Than loosed lipped dalliance can excite by wine

Or languid cadence; thy firm mouth could tell

Of ecstasies beyond the scale of song,

Where silence sweeps the cosmic chords of love,

Spirit with spirit subtly interfused,

Speech without language, wisdom without years,

Untrammelled, fearless, though the shoreless heights

Together ranging, in majestic joy,

These were our nuptials.

                    Thou didst promise once,

When first thy sovran voice rang through the mists

That cap these hilltops, and I felt the thrill

That bade me upward glance:—Wilt thou forget

That promise, for to give becomes a god,

And mortals need the gifts immortals give?

Grant then, dear goddess, this request of mine,

Redeem thy words, leave men their treachery;

Make me thy seer, and hide within my soul

The comfort of thy secret: though no more

Mine eyes may watch the pearl of thine approach,

Do not deceive me, else may I become

Irresolute and irrational and morose,

Or seek to lose myself in lower love,

Who now am filled with infinite content:

Thine image must not wither like a dream

When one awakes, nor vanish with the shapes

That filled my cloudland-boyhood long ago,

But throb for ever in this heart—thy home.

Fair are the forms of women; none like thine

Have stirred my soul with glorious energies

By subtle contact, when deep waves of joy

Roll their triumphant crests along the sand,

And flood this sense-bound shore, my body; ah!

If not with thee, yet in untrammelled vision

Alone, still let me feel the gods gaze down,

And breathe with us from their serene abodes;

So am I constant still if thou art kind,

For ever humble and for ever glad.

KEATS

Severn ! where is the bottom of such grief ?

Say ! what can calm my heart's tempestuous heat ?

These throbbing temples knock for Death's release,

Aye, that word Death's my only comfort now.

Say me not nay, nor strive to win me back,

Dark Charon's mantle flutters at my side,

And soon must Iris slit the slender thread

That binds me to this body.—Tell me, friend—

But no ! Give me the laudanum, give it me

I say ; this farce is deadening work for you !

Day after day to play the woman thus,

To feed, to nurse, to watch, night after night :

The case is hopeless, Severn, let me die,

What is the world to me or I to the world !

A dream, a dream—the fifth Act's far too long.

Severn, you are the only friend I have,

And you I hate to keep. What am I worth

That I should waste the hours your Art should
claim;

And yet you will not leave me, Severn? no,—

Am I in Rome?—the wonder of the world,

Necropolis of purpled conquerors,

Cradle of buried Cæsars.—Here are groves

Which Virgil and Mæcenas doubtless paced,

And shady porticoes which catch the North

Where Horace may have quaffed Falernian wine,

And praised his Sabine farm.—Am I in Rome?

And I must lie here dying and see nothing!

O dust, rebellious dust, so silent now.

Where be those patrons and their fleeting clients,

Patrician, pleb, tribune and senator?—

Vague names to fill a schoolboy's idle head.

Where be those gluttonous emperors, whose feasts

Amused my youth—and where those classic faces,

Warriors and statesmen, orators and poets,

Whose works and words the world has learnt
    by heart ?

Sooner or later we all come to this;

What's fame and name and grandeur?—Give us
    peace.

Play to me, Severn, that soft minuet

Of Haydn's soothed me much.—I seemed to see

A careful garden haunted by the dead,

Clipt yews and box-hedge, a long gravel-sweep

Of kissing chestnuts, and trim beds of flowers,

And a rosy arbour laced with eglantine,

And lilac fleeced with dew; and lawns of grass—

Green English lawns, so common everywhere;

But O, to one, whom sickness has stretched low,

How exquisite is e'en a blade of grass !

Alas, imagination will not stop :

I see a woman waiting for me there,

Her face out-pearls the moon, her locks of gold

Have leashed my straining soul, and these lorn orbs

Change colour gazing in those azure wells

Too deep for poet's praise; silence alone

And 'bated breath can give him strength to dive,

And sound the secret of his lady's eyes :

But I am weak—it was a cloud, a dream,

O God, let me not dream.

But look there, see,

A fairy lights the other taper, see !

That's merry, Severn, merry, 'tis indeed :

Alas ! how small a thing can please the sick.

Once—once I vowed the moon should be my bride,

The morning star my bright-hair'd seneschal,

Like passionless Hesperus, my soul should brood

On beauty, free from love's consuming fang ;

Pan my apostle, and stream-haunted woods

Our happy home,—but oh, that dream has fled.

For long or e'er the face of man was seen,

Beauty knew sorrow for her paramour,

And Nature's nuptials are not lightly made,

Nor brook man's arbitration ; with them, Death,

Concealed behind the flaming torch he held,

As patient as a shadow, stood unseen;

And as the pine torch wept, the shadow grew.

Has not some sculptor told the tale in stone ?

Ah ! Myths of Hellas ere mankind grew gray !

Ah ! Hierarchy of Gods Saturnian

That only haunt a poet's fancy now

Where are those manly forms of spring-tide strength

That tracked the fleet hart over dell and down,

Cheering their wild-eyed comrades to the chase

With bellowing horn; the wind-swept hills replying?

Lost are the gracile shapes of boy and girl,

Wood-nymph and shepherd fingering happy flowers,

Sweet pagan figures of the Pastoral !

Save haply, etched upon some potter's urn

They pipe to us of white simplicity,

The violet cloudlessness of Attic skies,

A world of hyacinth and glossy bee ;

In the morning of immortal loveliness

When summer filled the soul of Nature.—Gone,

Gone is that world's once naked innocence.

Why do we yearn for Hellas ?—Yet 'tis good

To have felt the potent force of Nature bend

Our weakness to her glory, and our poor hearts

Fire with her solemn torch—none bade me write :

There are no masters of that Art divine;

Only the Spirit scoffs and buffets us,

And some supreme ideal in the brain

Tells to the trembling hand what words to trace,

But oh, when traced, how vague, how nugatory :

Yet still we persevere, still hope to catch

Some fragment from the feast of harmony,

C

Though long or o'er the song our souls desire

Float down, death comes, life like a bubble breaks,

And men soon cease to know that we have lived.

And yet we need no pity. Nature breathes

Her consolation on her children, and

Comforts the o'er-fraught heart; on her relying,

The pageant of the world swims like a dream;

There never was true poet who fear'd death:

Rather we burst life's sensuous chrysalis

And greet the Angel's consummating touch

With mingled curiosity and awe.

Whether we sleep or live beyond, 'tis well,

What Nature hath ordained must needs be best.

The grandeur of a man is in his soul,

And how he faced the forces of the world,

And battled with himself—his tendency,

And not his finished work proclaim him great:

Did he maintain the majesty innate,

The inmost soundness, the inherent force

Of possible perfection in the race ?

Did he speak out the truth, and hint the path

Down which the coming generations, winged

With plumes of fiery hope, shall crowd and press ?

The glory of a poet is to stamp

An indelible mark of natural faith and love

Upon his epoch—this I have not done :

But I have lifted up the sacred hem

Of Nature's loveliness, and sung the truth

That dwells with beauty—more I might have done,

But full completion was denied me. So,

Whether men call me great, or scorn my work,

Rocked in the cradle of adversity,

I eased my soul of golden melodies,

And pointing to the gate called Beautiful,

Sleep,—Stretched at Nature's feet for evermore.

CHATTERTON'S DESPAIR

(Dedicated to J. A. S.)

This day of the week, tradition bids us know,

Died He who had no care to save Himself,

This day of the week will Thomas Chatterton die,

Having no care to live.

                        Had Barrett written

And sent me what I wished, had Beckford lived,

Or had the printers paid me what they owed,

Or had I owned one friend worthy the name,

I would not do this; hear me! in the future,

Printers and pimps should set up stock together,

For both are traffickers in human flesh

And prone to strangle immortality

By secret tricks of trade; listen and laugh!

Sixteen good songs for half-a-guinea cash;

Fell, Edmunds, Dodsley—all the crew of them,

Willing to tap my brains—Did Junius write?

I, Decimus, could match his stinging style,

And for that matter he's a purblind fool

Who cannot find a feasible argument

On either side, I found them sharp enough:

Since Churchill was in vogue, I had a fling

At satire too; the "County Magazine,"

"Middlesex Journal," "North Briton," "Freeholder,"

All knew me well enough:—Beside that work

Which claimed my deeper powers and grew in sleep.

O yes, I've struggled, but the dogs of Fate

Draw round their quarry, I am brought to bay:

Here in this dingy attic I must die:

Four months in London have I starved and sweated;

Hear me posterity! could a man do more

Than this boy did, or nurse a braver soul?

Only last month I spent my hard-earned pence

To send my mother and my sister something

Just as an earnest that I had that power,

Which given the chance, should lift us out of want

And they should live to praise the Bristol boy,

And share his fame.   O but my life has been

One brief ambitious stare : too proud to bend :

To crave a favour, stoop to menial toil,

Too proud: For to the mystic lady-Muse

I vowed myself a dauntless chevalier

From earliest childhood.   Has it led to this ?

Dost thou betray me, while thou let'st those live

In affluence, who fleer and desecrate

Thy godlike image?   Rise, thou haughty Sphinx,

Smite them, but let me soar.

              And I might soar,

Could I but stomach Mother Angel's tripe

Given me for charity, because she knows,

"I'm looking pinched : She will not press for pay,

Because she sees I'm poor," she says "and starved."

She bade me once " Go to and be a clerk,

And earn my bread like any honest lad,"

Sit like a monkey on a three legged stool,

And live by tottles! Pah! she turns me sick;

Her sweaty brow and fat square podgy fingers

Greasy with cooking, make me shudder: Ah!

'Tis strange this psychic hand should have to waste,

While hers grows red with plenty: she has that ,

While I must sup on this which now I take.

—Not yet, let's reason.

Thoughtful Seneca,

Brutus and Cassius, Romans, perished thus;

Thus Cato, stern and calm: So Chatterton

Crushes his agony with stoicism—

For there's a limit which man's fortitude

Of suffering can endure; but past that point,

The affronted will disdaining to be shackled,

Dungeon'd too deep in dreadful misery,

Finds a sure freedom by another way,

And none but brave men dare to tread that way.

I will not weep, nor cry: "For pity's sake,

Give the young Poet bread,"—I want no pity,

For to need pity is a pitiful thing,

And mark of mean birth. No! I will lie down

Unconquered. Even the weakest woman knows

There are some snares more terrible than death,

A captain scorns to quit his sinking ship,

Dishonour slays a soldier more than death;

And I, shall I submit? Never! Needs then

I fare to-night where hunger cannot hunt me,

And where the sting of pride is never felt,

And vain the lust of self-idolatry:

Fame's herald cannot parley at those walls,

Nor shake the gates of everlasting sleep;

Come death! Thou seneschal of rebel dust,

That wait'st on all, in turn. Not yet, not yet,

Let me pull back the blind and seek a sign:

Alas! the skies are very pitiless,

God seems quiescent, and those stelléd fires

Are void of comfort for me; all is blank,

Nescient of sympathy and desolate.

Mercy! how have I made what fatal error,

How lost the thread in life's dark labyrinth

To stumble on this den?

               Come, I will dream,

And memory shall mock at misery,

And beauty share with hunger all I have.

This mouldy attic vanishes: I feel

The sharp salt wind go whistling past my ears;

I'm on the gorge at Clifton; far below

The sluggish Avon crawls, on th' other side

A forest frowns the sun goes down behind : •

Behold me in my yellow stockings stand,

And garb of Charity. O cursèd Fate!

An antique soul lodged in a stripling's frame,

What care I now? is not thought free as death?

The wizard twilight holds me with a spell;

I seem to see great warriors in the air,

Mail-clad, on wingéd coursers snorting fire,

I their magician; when I give command,

They wheel and charge, or fall into the deep;

And far away to the West looms a vast band,

Deep-dyed in sunset robes, half-gods, half-men,

Harping of chivalry and battles old,

The castled pageantry of feudalism,

Cathedral pomp and monkish vespers swelling,

Rent standards flushed with many a bloody fight,

In glorious hurly-burly; while my soul

Glows o'er the grand confusion, and is calm.

What are the prizes of small life to me,

The pitiful tricks, the narrow shallow limits

Of the mean pence-clutching mediocrity

In the town below; when at the freak of will,

I'm lord of legions and the realms of thought?

Master of these, I scorn that lower world.

Must I bow down before the Juggernaut

Of Mammon? No, who will may temporise,

And wear a Janus-face,—but I cannot.

Let me go further back : a different scene :

The nearer to the dawn the greater hope :

But twelve years old, yet hard at work at home

In my own attic, where with parchments old

From Canynge's Cofre, books and chemicals,

I the young Faustus toil'd ; O happy days,

With none to break upon my reverie,

While hour by hour on Redcliffe opposite

Towering I gazed ; till antique images

Of monk and warrior marshalled in my brain,

A secret birth I would not deign divulge.

Shall I forget that evening ? while I worked,

My sister knocked, I would not let her in ;

She said, " A letter for you ;" up I jumped,

Unlocked the door sufficient for my arm

Thrust through, to seize it ; and as I broke the seal,

I swore from sheer excitement. 'Twas from Walpole.

Here was the friend, the heaven-sent friend I craved,

The courtier-wit, the learned man of letters,

Whose kindly hand might help an aspiring youth;

Bristol should never hold me after this,

To London, to London, throbbed my heart.—I've
    come,

I've seen, I starve—but Walpole lives!

O bed whereon I fall no more to rise,

Posterity shall judge who is the forger,

My lips are silent, justice is not here.

I'll not repent, defiant to the death,

For what I could I did and I have lived.

O double world, so hard to harmonise!

Eighteen brief summers is enough, I'm tired,

And very very hungry, but not mad.

Come to my bedside, mother, your boy is dying

Alone; O take my hand and close mine eyes,

O cruel world! you cannot hurt me now.

Bristol is far away, and home, dear mother !

Alas ! I was not all a son might be,

But you could never understand my ways,

And no one understood—they called it pride.

It may be I shall wake and live again,

And love, and Heaven forgive.   But who can tell ?

Delusion, and delusion, and delusion,

It may be death is a delusion too !

Farewell !   You'll live, for you were never proud.

   Will he not come home again ?

      No, he is dead,

      Gone to his death-bed,

   All under the willow-tree.

IN THE SHADOW OF THE CHURCH

Turn, my beloved, let me speak a word.

Katherine, the die is cast, and day is done;

No tears! in silence let our last farewell

Be taken, for it is most weak to mourn

For that which hath no remedy but death.

I'll not repent, what have we to repent?

While life is life, and love life's lonely prize,

Why should we weep that we have won that prize,

Though but to lose it? as a flower that withers

At sunrise. Go!—but do not go : still, still,

Would I enfold thee in mine arms, and rain

Salt tears till all creation swim in mist.

Would I might die with gazing on thee, Katherine.

God made me man but man hath made me monk,

God made thee mine, but man hath come between,

So runs this transient episode away,

Love's labour lost ; home, home, a ruined hope.

My dreams lie buried in the wilderness,

Joys scattered on the barren dunes of time,

Proud thought o'erthrown—and beauty doom'd to
dust.

Thine hazel eyes will haunt me in my sleep,

Thy form swim twixt the chalice and the cross,

Thy brown hair touch my cheek, when bowing low

In fast and supplication, I implore

Mercy for sins that I have never known.

Go to thy homestead duties, I to prayer

And lonely cell and austere vows must turn,

To pore on ancient missal, and the Word,

And mutter misereres for the dead.

Did not the holy Master claim too much,

The impossible ? O what most haggard deeds

Hath not religion been persuasive of ?

I would I were a painter for thy sake

To limn thy face above the chancel, there

To smile for ever with the holy Babe

Upon thine arm, of motherhood divine,

Worshipped by thousands with adoring palms;

Alas, no art is mine, only the pang,

And endless pity for thy withered youth,

For thou wilt never wed, though I am gone :

Sundered and silent, time will soon flow by.

Thine eyes are shells still trembling with the spray

Of seas celestial, flung by envious waves

Upon these temporal coasts; soon, when the tide

Rolls up, they will be gathered back again,

And sink once more into the deep unknown;

Whence issuing once, they told a wanderer

Of other lands and seas beyond the sun.

Life hath two scales, one Mammon's and one God's;

And when this is depressed, then that is raised;

The heavy cross flung in the fleshly scale

Will lift thy soul to strike the stars on high,

So art thou nearest heaven in deepest woe,

Gethsemane's the porch of paradise;

Katherine, farewell, the trial of faith is ours.

Katherine, farewell, still silent.—God is Love.

LINES ON AN OLD MAN READING

He sits in his arm-chair;
Sunk are his eyes, and somewhat dulled perchance;
The features scored and trenched with many a furrow,
Scars in life's battle, now to end so soon:
Scanty his locks and white: his clothes hang loose:
Creased his hand-veins and swollen; all the marks
Of powers fast-failing recognisable:
And yet he reads, with one foot in the grave:
And round that snow-capped hive the busy bees
Of thought still hum: and with the month's fresh
    flowers
Crowd the o'er brimming brain-cells, e'er the frost
Of winter warn that working-time is done.
Why such activity then? for we may guess
That none on earth shall share this aftermath,

In the world's busy mart his place is filled:

" Peace for the old," they say, " with meditation ;

For us new generations, yours is past."

And yet he reads ; and will none benefit ?

Mere waste, mere plethora of Nature's store?

But in the old man's face there shines a light:

" I still am younger than you think, my friends :

And trust the instinct, for God does not jest.

It may be, when my twilight closes in,

And bees no longer hum around this hive,

But dormant lie in seeming death, and feed

On the sweet labour of the summer months ;

That I, like them, shall find good use for all,

Nothing superfluous, mere pass-time nothing.

It may be I shall need my knowledge then,

And in new worlds act out experience here ;

For all God's works rise on a gradual scale,

From good to better, and from better best :

Doubtless our use of life here must determine

Our station in the next—if next there be.

The economy of Nature will not waste,

Cannot afford to waste, one man's good hive ;

Here being needed, for a while I stayed,

That there, being needed, I may win a place,

And work my way through progress infinite.

I'm not so old as you suppose, dear friends ;

Though I must leave you, and with some regret,

And one world at a time is the wise plan ;

Still I conceive no reasonable doubt

But that these cells shall pour earth's honey forth,

And in the fadeless fields of asphodel

Barter therewith for other honey, good

Alike for them, as their's will be for me ;

From nothing, nothing comes. Wherefore, my friends,

Ply with your busiest wing from flower to flower :

Store up, store up, fill your capacious hives,

And garner knowledge while the sun is yours ;

Aye till the curfew toll 'tis not too late:

Perchance, the last blithe truant laden down

With nectar, while the rest are snugly housed,

May bring the costliest essence of them all,

Whom to have lost had been great detriment."

ON THE MULTIPLICITY OF POETS

"A locust-plague of poets now," one cries :—
"As grains of Lybian sand innumerable."
"Countless as the billows of Atlantic seas
That arch their scornful crests where no shore breaks
The grandeur of their limitless succession."

The critic groans "He cannot drain the sea:"
But better thus : "Profound Immensity !
Loved boom of sullen thunder in mine ear !
That trumpet of defiance to the winds
Which only deep and massive waters blow,
Is born of drops of salt confederate :
O who could wish a breaker less? e'en bells
Of foam that scud before the rousing breeze,
Vacantly irridescent, hint the stress

And strife of pushing waters underneath,

While e'en the third-wave breaks incontinent :

But where's the loss ? Old Neptune still roars on.

Just so the complex choir of Britain now,

Say rather of the world's democracy,

Is grander in its multiplicity

Than any single voice of simpler days :

Sweet was the oaten pipe Sicilian,

Matchless the plastic plainness of the Greek,

Meek Maro's tender majesty ; the swoop

Of him whose phœnix-dust Ravenna guards,

How swift, how final ! Never has the voice.

Of singing ceased since that eventful dawn

Which smiled upon the jocund company

Of pilgrims bound for Canterbury :—But

Cephissus, Tiber, Arno, Thamesis,

Now blend their rich-ored individual streams

With the sad thunders of a coastless sea :

One everlasting oratorio

Born of slow-heaving waters submarine,

Of multitudinous waves, and buoyant billows,

Of scum, of broken surf, and tossing crest,

Mounts up, breathed from the common heart of all ;

And Neptune laughs to hear his children sing.

So let the sea-cow bark.

RURAL LIFE IN ENGLAND

By John Self, Rhapsodist.

1

I'll tell you how our village looks
In England at the summer prime,
My knowledge is not gleaned from books,
Or abstract thoughts of the sublime :
No ! but by communing and prayer,
From hour to hour, from day to day,
During the magic month of May,
With Nature in the open air.

2

E'en now the bursting blaze of gold
Blinds my weak eyes with dizziness ;
I see the champaign fold on fold
Panting with bliss and loveliness ;

England! dear garden of the North,

Whose sons are feudal, silent, proud,

Lords of the earth by all allowed,

She rears them here and flings them forth.

3

At dawn,—the window open wide—

The thrush, the cuckoo, and the lark,

By many a singer deified,

Are heard in every field and park,

No touch of grief is in their tone;

But should you hear the nightingale

Plead low to the stars, and pause, and wail,

You'd feel how men still suffer wrong.

4

In May the chestnut's stalwart bough

Builds up its pyramid of light,

The first to leaf, the first to strow

Its sailing petals left and right,

The bower of many a missel-thrush :

Then, too, the lilac white and grey,

Bursts, blossoms, weeps, and fades away,

Scenting the air at sunset-flush.

❧　　　*　　　*　　　*　　　*

5

I see the red-roof'd cottages,

The smoke curls up—how blue and straight—

To-morrow will be fine, it says,

Or should be fine ; at any rate

'Tis better not to dogmatise :

The swallows skim the cattle-pool

Where cows are standing sleek and cool,

Flicking their tails to scare the flies.

6

There is a fragrant smell of milk,

Mingled with wafts of wild dog-rose,

Sweeter to me than all the silk

In which my scented lady goes :

Where is the city's boasted charm ?

Take all the treasures of the realm,

Give me a hawthorn and an elm

And health upon an English farm.

7

The villagers, when work is done,

And when the thickening twilight lends

A beauty to the setting sun,

Loiter around the corner ends,

Smoking and gossiping at ease,

Their brains are never overwrought

Or harassed with religious thought,

They live and die in frugal peace.

8

The sombre yew-trees close at hand,

That guard the barrows of the dead,

Preach lessons all can understand,

Though beauty robs them of their dread :

The common course—the common fate—
The churchyard grass is wet with showers,
And bees are busy in the flowers
That mark the term of man's estate.

9

Death stamps a prescient majesty
Even upon the brow of want,
Death binds by ties of sympathy
The learned and the ignorant :
The proud Patrician lined with gold,
The Peasant-labourer in his blouse,
Meet, massed in death's impartial house,
And recognise a common mould.

10

The pride of race is being spent,
Democracy is taking shape,
And he who boasts of long descent
Is only nearer to the ape.

Let brother take his brother's hand,

And own we are of equal stock,

Nature can build a rampart-rock,

By welding grains of simple sand.

11

What makes the splendour of the field ?

'Tis not a solitary flower,

The waste of time to which men yield

Lies not in any single hour:

A drop of rain is not a shower:

A man,—be he however proud—

Is still but one among a crowd,

It is the mass that makes the power.

*   *   *   *   *

12

Many a half-hour one may pass,

Stretched in the meadow at full ease,

Amid a countless sea of grass,

Slow, undulating in the breeze:

Imagination unconfined

Here proudly mounts where will may lead,

Can make a cloud an Arab steed,

And gallop with the rushing wind.

13

A touch of Nature's magic wand

Moves thoughts of manlier majesty

Than all the learning of the land:

Simplicity's enough for me:

To catch the wild lark's morning call,

Or take a solitary jaunt

To hear, beneath some leafy haunt,

The streamlet's flowing madrigal.

14.

Long, long, too long I've felt the weight

Upon me of the cultured age,

Now with a shout, I spring elate,

And claim my lawful heritage:

Let poets file their dainty words,

And filigree their Watteau-phrases;

I sit and wanton with the birds,

And sing among the summer daisies.

15

Nature, divinest Mother, so

May strength with undisturbed repose

Attend me whereso'er I go,

And calmness bring at evening-close:—

And grant, ere thy enshadowing wing

Close o'er the twilight of my days,

That I once more may sing thy praise

With worthier imagining.

SEEDS OF PROGRESS

By John Self, Rhapsodist.

The wind was warm to-day, and smelt of spring,

The sea as faint with some long reverie,

(Her white limbs still half flushed with ecstasy

From the sun's lordly revels) slept secure,

Only one handmaid-seagull hovered near

To tend the sleeping queen—yet not alone

The ocean, but the land itself looked fair:

I know that buds will break on every bough,

And hope lend lustre to the tender blade,

E'en now along the thicket I descry

The noiseless midges weaving their airy loom;

Joy throbs their tiny hearts; the rooks are loud,

And lesser starlings fly innumerable

Across the labour of the plough, to peck

Food from the new-turned glebe; all birds are glad,

E

A tantivy of gray pigeon from yon holt

Clap the warm light, pursuing and pursued.

O mother, mother, why this mystery?

Have I not served thee well?—and yet so mute!

Love's tears will dim thine April violet,

The flossy bud of primrose hear the brook

And wake with spring, aye, every stick and straw

Will feel th' exultant thrill, and welcome give.

Shall I alone forget thee, and be mute,

Pass by in silence? Ah! I know not why,

The dawn of beauty is akin to pain,

And love doth wake in fear, no sensuous shaft

So poignant as the arrowy glance of spring.

Why do such mornings stir sad memory,

O why the bird's sweet note, unbidden tears?

What would'st thou have me cry, dear mother, speak!

My heart is pure to listen, quick to catch

Thy subtle whispers—may I say a word?

I did not come from nothing as ye know,

I am a part of what I see around,

For all I see seems to my inner sight

Arrested man—and thus my love expands

Till aspiration kindles into act,

And act reacts in wider sympathy

With all that is. The timeless distances

That loom behind the least make him appear

Both small and great : small in the sum of things,

And great as having that to use at will,

Which millions of long years have gone to make.

I am not as an evening nightingale

That sings of sorrow all alone, and flings

Her solitary song away in haste,

And drops in silence with the shrivell'd leaf ;

If I am strong, my strength is also yours,

If I am joyful, you will share that joy,

The past has sown the flower that springs to-day,

A plain meek man who cannot be dismissed.

The great world-spirit seems to chant again,

The pulse of poetry to stir anew

To grander issues; if it once seemed good

To lock a fairy in a lonely line,

To carve a crystal cameo; now no more :

Dazed are mine eyes, my throat too thick for speech,

Good bye to fancy, give me fact instead,

The bald and terrible scientific fact,

This fills me with a hope that transcends all,

A hope, an insight, aye, a certainty !

Ha! for the rose's blood beats in my blood,

The beasts my cousins, and the birds my kin,

With every tiny elemental wing

I claim connection; for the world streams on,

Creation does not falter, all that is

Strains forward and improves from day to day,

A grand and infinite complexity

Based on broad unity of cosmic law,

No split, no sundering, but resistless force

Working in solemn order, upward ever ;

Why pant ? why hurry ? what is there to fear ?

Man's imperfections lessen day by day,

The chariot of the world's democracy

Wheels slowly on ; the pigmy Phaethon

Who held the reins of Empire for a day,

Drops headlong ; but Apollo never falls.

Think you that God in Piccadilly dwells,

Or yawns from clubland on wet afternoons,

A varnished cynic shod in patent shoes,

Grown weary somewhat of the ways of men ?

No, no, the kingdom of the poor draws nigh,

The Philistine is on thee dandy Dick,

Look to thy brains and not thy pedigree ;

For the workman stares his master in the face,

And those who sat in darkness see a light,

And there is something in the souls of men

That cannot be down-trampled, nor bought up,

Nor patronised, nor pauperised, nor scorned,

And woe to those who will not recognise

That something; for it does not dwell in one,

But in the race : Nature is prodigal,

And will attain her end at any cost.

The sky's no longer like a crystal case,

With a circling sun to warm the good flat earth,

And man as master; nor the stars no more

Mere points of flame to light the bell-man home ;

Things were not made merely for man's desire,

To serve his ends : his minion or his thrall.

"Break me my heavens," quoth God, "and let
    me see

Their boasted glory shrivel in the gaze

Of world on world, innumerable, proud,

Swifter than sight, whereof their pigmy earth

Swims like a bubble (albeit of my breath)

Upon the waters of the universe.

Ha, these upstanding men that seem so great,

Of magnet atoms marvellously moulded,

They shall grow greater by another fall.

Witless you laughed, you killed my herds and flocks,

You raised yourselves an inch above the rest,

And made your God, a man ; my world, a board

To serve your appetites ; enough of this.

Know now you cannot kill a jot of mine,

My power fails not, no atom ever dies,

It cannot die, for I am in that atom ;

My progress marches on with steady foot

To certain triumph ; the music of my laws

Your ephemeral thunder mocks, you wake to sleep :

And pass like shadows wailing bitterly,

Cramped in your cast-iron creeds, until some flame

Heat the same atoms to another shape :

Then shouting you proclaim, " Behold the truth,"

But truth is meek and comes not with a shout."

The spirit of democracy is mild,

Wise without learning, full of sympathy,

Has no desire to quarrel about creeds,

Wishes none ill as long as they will work;

All work's the same with her, no small nor great

Her heart expands and is not envious,

Her soul as ancient as the naked stars,

As unashamed as Nature.   'Tis her joy

Not to decry the storied majesty

Of saint and hero, king and conqueror,

The pomp and pageantry of feudalism,

The cloistered lady, the romantic love;

But she refuses to regard the world

As satan-bound, and sinful at the core:

Rather she feels God breathe through everything,

Making and moulding all to His good end;

And all men help him who do honest work.

For 'tis the man that consecrates the deed,

And not the deed that magnifies the man.

Democracy has no desire to slay,

Does not pull down, but rather levels up,

And wants no prizes in another world :

" O in this life " she cries " life to the full,

And quench the thirst of curiosity ;

The costliest foe of man is ignorance."

Wherefore, chant forth, my soul, in faith and love ;

And mix thy rivulet with the rushing river,

In the great whirl of things take thou thy place :

For now the night of sorrow dies away,

And creed and caste are melted in one flood

That rolls its mighty billows, crest and foam,

And tonnage of tremendous waters, on,

Till God's democracy emerge at last

Self-governed, self-controlled, speaking one speech,

Slaves of the lamp of love, and therefore free.

FERDINAND

A quiet wash of water; moon, and miles of sand;
Horror of solitude; God, Death, and Ferdinand.

"Hear me, Thou Lord of life! For am I not thy
   child?

Hear me, by whatsoever name best reconciled:

Prime Force, Creative Cause, Jehovah, Great
   Unknown,

I cry, waste-bound I cry, alone with Thee alone.

The waves' hoarse diapasons mock me. Who am I?

Sperm-germ of cuckoo-spittle—Man—O let me die.

For oh, to what vain end would art strain out
   life's tether?

Tis but a little folding of the hands together.

What of the night?   Speak, watchman-star!"—
   "The night will pass,

And morning break:"—"and wax and wane: all
  flesh is grass!

In vain I tread the crowded square, I pace the
  wild,

To find one human face, calm, perfect, undefiled.

I see but incarnated shards and shreds of lust,

Legions of lost souls, hungry miracles of dust.

Oh for ablution." As he spake, he moved to meet

Ocean: white tongues of surf broke hissing round
  his feet.

"'Tis O for a new creation, a dream that we have
  not dreamt,

A life of manifold action, if any were worth the
  attempt.

Novelty, novelty, aye, till everything novel must
  seem

But infinite variations thrummed on a threadbare
  theme.

For the tale of the earth is told, and girdled the
  earth's strait scope :

The fabled chest is exhausted, and science has
strangled hope.

Automatons all as it seems, in body, in will, and
in mind :

Destiny handles the tiller : necessity sits in the wind.

We compete and defeat one another: we labour
and know too much :

Our passions are frittered in folly till deadened is
Nature's touch.

The Apple of Love is eaten green ; we are flaccid
ere ripe,

We huddle and bubble together, till we trend to a
pigmy type.

We force and we forge our children to gather
untimely fruit :

To know if the brain be growing, we pluck it up
by the root.

And most are as grasping as feeble ; methinks that
there is not one

Who dare read by the inward lamp, or will suffer
and stand alone.

I hate this base generation of baby-egos and boys,

This mart of mouthing and mammon, of belial-
babble and noise :

This age of smatter and smartness, of cunning
shallow and 'cute,

Where the silt of civilization scarce covers the
naked brute.

But thou, dread death, art firm: turning to thee,
we cease."

Slow swell'd th' voluptuous wave, and coil'd and
pluck'd his knees.

"O to see a new sun rising out beyond some unknown bay,

O to hear the wild birds singing far away, and far
away :

Watch the planets flush at twilight over some
marmoreal sea,

Muse upon the cosmic vision where no fool can
follow me.

O my soul is lost in sorrow, sick with sighing
for mine own,

And my cry to God and man is simply to be left
alone.

Will they never cease to bicker, bite and blacken,
fret and fume ?

O to hear the trump of God blare out their
everlasting doom !

I should laugh to see their fulsome vices
hypocritical,

Like the masks from actors' faces when the play is
over, fall :

Scan them naked and astounded, know them as
they really are,

See their pseudo-philanthropics weighed before the
judgment bar :

I should smile to see the man who sneers and
cavils at the throne,

Battens on the sins of others, strive to justify
his own :

See the journalistic braggart curl up like a
frightened louse,

See the editorial ' we ' shrink back as modest as
a mouse :

See the pariah and the pauper, see the outcast
in her shame,

Stand above the worldly-wise man, step before the
stately dame :

Would the heavens might sink in thunder, stars
splash, earth and ocean gape,

That the gods might close for ever th' annals of
the human ape.

Alas, vain is this loud lament—vain these sighs."

And now the rising sea plunged heavily round his
thighs.

"O that I had not been born into this æon of
arid woe,

O that I had lived and flourished half a thousand
years ago.

In an age when life was joyous, somewhere in
the sunny south,

When a passionate love of beauty passed in song
from mouth to mouth.

Would that I could quit the stricken city, and
in lieu of woes,

Lie enchanted in the golden garden of Boccaccio's ;

Laughing at his tales of frolic with their sly
  insouciance,

Loll at listless ease, and eat the lotus-leaf of
  indolence :

Vernal maidens such as Botticelli painted would
  be there,

Sprightly as a host of lilies, breeze-blown lilies
  debonair.

Lo ! I seem to see before me in a vision at my feet,

All the youth and yeast of Florence masquerading
  in the street.

See them pass ! their reeling flambeaux stream
  against a sallow sky :

Dainty comfits, darts of cupid fall in showers
  incessantly :

Posies toss'd from tinsell'd casements pelt the
  surging crowd below :

Damsels borne on milk-white palfreys, nodding
  gaily as they go :

Frescobaldi, Soderini, Salviati—all are there—

Private feuds are drowned in revel, naught is
  banished now but care.

'Hail Lorenzo! Lord of freedom: Hail Lorenzo!
he is ours,

Welcome May, the month of madness! Florence
hails the month of flowers.'

'Hail Lorenzo!' Lute and cymbal clash and echo
from afar:

Gallants dight in silken doublets follow his
triumphal car.

O'er the bridge while Arno trembles to the cresset's
fitful flare;

See! the dome of Brunelleschi shadows half the
central square.

'We defy thee, death, thou dotard! while our merry
pageant goes:

Haste, haste, carnival is passing. Pluck the lily,
strip the rose.

Haste! the spool of time is turning: Maidens,
make no long delay,

From the tangled floss of Fortune spin the
brightest thread ye may.'

Voice by voice, the minstrels catch and lift the
measure as they go,

F

While the lyric-shuttle weaves the web of music
to and fro.

O'er S. Marco, shriller fragments, as the choric
voices swell,

Smite Savonarola brooding lonely in his cloistered
cell."

"But such pageants ceased. And Florence was
not merry any more :

All her wild hozannas silenced by the cannon's
shattering roar.

So, youth's democratic fancies, passionate visions
of redress,

Pass like pictures. Hemm'd and harass'd stands
he silent in the press.

Poor and disenchanted : now he seeks for
sympathy in one,

Marries in a blind delusion : wakes to find himself
alone.

Vainly he maligns his fortune; pressing wants
and cares obtrude,

And the fight for sheer existence scarcely leaves
him space to brood.

All his soul's lustrous enamel, all th' ideal's pink
veneer,

Rubbed and worn away by living in the city, year
by year.

Thwarted by a thousand worries, petty pothers,
paltry strife,

Selfishness at last becomes the ruling motive of
his life.

Cased and crusted in convention; pillar of a
palsied church :

All his nobler speculations left for ever in the
lurch :—

Aye, we know the type of pillar, plethoric with
dews of grace,

Unctuous pillars, whitewashed pillars, bald and
broadest at the base !—

Now he ridicules his earlier vision of a perfect state,

Prides himself on being purely practical—and never
late !

Late ! ah me, the ways of mortals seem so sad,
so comical !

I can scarcely weep for laughing, laugh for
weeping at it all.

Pitiful pathos, fierce philippic; which is timelier,
who can say?

While we watch the rising waters wash the sands
of time away.

Oh, my soul, thou ancient river, thou hast
trodden down man's strength:

Aye, that ancient river Kishon rolls us all away at
length.

Harrying, hurrying, marrying, burying, where's the
wonder, where's the worth?

Comes at last the staid procession, sable steeds,
and dropping earth.

Ah! these spaces stretched above me seem
surcharged with speechless fate,

Ah! this scintillating, silver, shimmering sea
disconsolate!

Man might be a king of beauty, man might fill
a god-like throne,

Could he learn himself to choose the law of nature
for his own.

But we imitate a copy, dare not be ourselves at all;

Or we deviate from nature, just to seem original.

O ye sapphire chasms of splendour, tell me
whither, tell me whence;

Shout the answer, echo, echo—I defy the
consequence."

But from the void vast night rang out no answering
note,

Albeit the bubbling tide had risen, and lapp'd his
throat.

"Out of the east and the west swell the sounds
of disconsolate wailing,

Wailing of infinite woe: sounds of interminate
sighs.

For the heart of half of the human race is a prey
to delusion:

Ignorance, mother of sin, rules in the street and
the square.

Round and around like a mill-wheel the nations
from sunrise to sunset

Toil; and a turmoil of tears is life; and death is
a sleep.

I know, if stayed, I too like a straw should go
    down in the maelstrom :

Therefore with soul undefiled turn I, dear mother,
    to thee.

Out of the ivory gate have the sanguine illusions
    of boyhood

Fled : but a dawn of despair breaks in this desolate
    town.

Thousands of cynical swords, and legions of
    devils beleaguer,

Banners and brass of the strong storm round this
    sorrowful fort.

Alas! there are traitorous curs too that lurk in
    the citadel smiling,

Whispering, " Better to yield, better surrender
    than starve ! "

Nay, by the deeds of the dead. I swear that I will
    not surrender,

Therefore, inviolate death, turn I for refuge to thee.

" I will open the wicket of sleep, I will pass to the
    garden of Lethe,

Under the trees I will stretch, hearing the
nightingale sing.

Where the winds and the waves sweep never, nor
sign nor season revolving

Comes: but immutable calm rules, a perpetual
queen.

Under the boughs of the broad crepuscular cedar
of silence,

Couched upon sorrel and rue, lost in monotonous
gloom :

Alone, I will ponder at dreamful ease where the
shadows lie longest ;

Marked from the boisterous crowd—waiting and
watching alone.

Nor folly, nor fever, nor fret, nor favour of
fortune shall find me

There, where the hemlock flowers whiten and wither
intact.

Flush in the fruit, and bloom from the bud, and
the falling of blossom

Pass, but no change is felt. Summer and winter
are one.

Quiet security rests like a spell o'er the spot, and consummate

Silence sombre, and deep shade, and incurious sleep.

"Courage ! ere I pass for ever let me chant a palinode.

Some by right are heirs of Belial, some are saints and sons of God.

Some are born to sink in sin, and some are framed to shield and save ;

Æons of ancestral influence make and mould us from the grave.

Aye, and living, mere suggestion can induce a waking trance,

And another guide our motive, lord of life and circumstance.

But the puppet, self deluded, poses as a freeman still,

Speaks of sudden intuitions, while he serves a stronger will.

What is overmastering genius but an automatic strain

Of the racial instinct somehow summed up in a
single brain ?

Many a link of dead endeavour joins the genius
to the dunce,

And he reaps in rich abundance seed another
scattered once.

Every kindred aspiration, every effort of the mind,

Goes to swell the consummation of the mission of
mankind.

Not a sin, a vice is useless; no experience but
must tend

By accumulated wisdom somehow to the wished-for
end.

As the Israelites of old went journeying onward
with the ark ;

Genius plants the human standard furlongs further
through the dark.

He alone, or some few with him, sees by night
the pillar of fire ;

And his eyes reflect that glory : dead : his ashes
still inspire.

" In the hour of deep disaster, when the cry is
' Ichabod ' ;

Flash of faith. A single strong man. Nations thunder where he trod.

From the Jews' fell persecutions sprang the world's white aloe-flower:

Prophets, monarchs, priests, and martyrs prayed and passioned for that hour.

When He came: He was rejected, scorned His summons from above,

Hunted like a lonely partridge was the Lord of light and love.

True to-day the mediocre do not murder any more,

True, the Sadducean critics serve statistics, not the law!

So they cry: ' He's mad or mattoid, genius is akin to crime:'

Baby-savans, blasé cynics stab and sneer him out of time.

By the great ones gone before us, better freedom though in death;

Than to fester in the city breathing in another's breath.

I will tell the shades in Sheol: 'Merry England is no more,

Only smoke and squalid millions, miles of brick and mud galore!'

Faith has vanished from our faces: in this life alone, it seems,

Must the wise man lay up treasure: and forsake fanatic dreams.

Give us truth, whate'er the ransom for truth's freedom we must pay:

Yet I think our mothers were not wrong to teach us how to pray.

There a mystery unexplained still, and I hear it on the beach,

Ceaseless in these surf-tongues hissing at the seaweed out of reach.

From the deeper seas, an echo: 'Seeds are scattered everywhere,

And a soul of sterner fibre shall be born of thy despair.'

Ah! indeed, the individual withers, as the poet sings;

We must die content to grasp the righteous tendency of things :

Though so loath to hear the phantom knocking on the other side ;

We must pass. and let the others blunder where we used to guide.

Some-day, doubtless, somehow, though we shall not live to see that day,

Man's immortal aspirations will be summoned into play.

When our so-called education will not leave him, like a child,

Naked of bread-winning knowledge, hungry in a pathless wild.

When the curse of competition branded on the young man's brow

Will not find him old at thirty, as it often finds him now.

When the statesman will not turn the public trust to private ends,

Nor the homeless needy lady have to live upon her friends.

When the woman and the man shall stand as comrades side by side:

When to help, not hoard the million, will be held in highest pride.

When a conscientious thinker will not have to quit his church,

Nor the callow curate clamour, like a parrot, from his perch.

When distracted sects shall widen and unite in love and zeal,

Christ identified at last with our humanity's ideal !

All these things will happen some day, in the future far ahead,

Some day in the golden future, after you and I are dead.

O to live and love again when æons shall have washed us clean,

When this stormy world has wheeled into a cycle more serene !

As for this, my Roman exit, let him judge who understands.

God! if God there be: I give my body and soul
into Thy hands."

A splash. A string of bubbles. A widening ring.
No more.

Only a quiet wash of water on the shore.

A DEMOCRATIC CHANT

By John Self, Rhapsodist.

Behold! I will sing one great song from the depths
of my soul;

Of life : what it was, what it is, what it may be,—
the whole :

Not muffled with vague lamentation, not stammered
in rage :

Not beating void wings like a bird at the bars of
her cage :

Nor gazing with eyes from dim watching made sore
and distressed,

Not with burden of years of long labour and learning
oppressed ;

But buoyant, as after a lapse of unsorrowful rest

On the lap of our wonderful mother. whose beautiful
breast

Lulls all her tired offspring to slumber with gentle
caress,

Who loves not her mighty ones more, nor her little
    ones less,

So impartial is she from whose temporal prison I
    break,

As free as from rock spouts a torrent, white-flashing,
    awake,

In joy of wild liberty leaping in headlong career,

Too strong to be stemmed, too liquid to pause, too
    swift to be clear,

But with frolic of foam-bell and froth and impetuous
    voice,

He cries to the highlands and lowlands: I flow,
    I rejoice;

For the spell of the morning is on me, the mist of
    the heights:

From the womb of the mountain I spring, from
    impervious nights

In the dim underworld of deep darkness; where,
    pent and at bay,

Meand'ring in mazy abysses, I forced my slow way

Through slate, slag, and shale: till behold! I leap
    forth into day.

I ask not for smoothness, for idlesse: broad
  boulders may block,

Pen, parcel and split: I accept them; with many
  a rude shock

And buffet of cliff, I race forward somehow to mine
  end,

Nor loiter to question and quibble whereto 'tis
  I tend;

For the weight of my waters impels me resistlessly
  on

'Neath the sunlight of labour, the magic of twilight,
  of moonlight alone;

I swirl the green banks of broad meadows and
  champaigns of corn,

Through forests of firs and through dingles and
  dells where the birds sing at dawn,

Through great lone recesses, and chasms of un-
  speakable gloom,

'Twixt drizzling black rock-reefs I gather with
  thunder, and boom,

When all the blind bulk of my passion is hurled
  forth apace,

G

(A polished white column of waters arched over
    sheer space),

Ere fountains of foam are dashed back again,
    shattered in spray :

But I shake my stunned senses, recover, and urge
    on my way :

Soon streamlet and burn, tarn and beck, bend
    their footsteps to me,

My brothers, my comrades, they join me, they
    long for the sea :

Though our sources be many, and voices may
    differ—in purpose and love

With one soul to one sea democratic united we
    move :

And who shall resist us persisting, who bind us,
    who block ?

They who cannot and dare not encounter are
    welcome to mock :

They may stand on the bank, wring their hands
    in despair, watch and weep,

And wail for the past that has flashed by for ever,
    may wail for the steep,

Whence our waters first rose, the pure well-head, the fountain, the source :

And others may fear for the future, the close of the course ;

For already the waters are salt with the tears of the ages, and dull

With the turbulent billows of passion, blind pushing, and clamour: and full

Of the poison and reek of the mills, and the filth of the towns :

Oh ! what can the future avail, though they court us and crown us with crowns,

If the waters we drink are mephitic, the flood that we float on debased,

With all the morn's innocent dimple and shimmer and dancing effaced !

Well ! so let them wail as they will, if their faith be declined :

Yet still, O the grandeur of dust, the incredible marvel of mind :

Outracing the gale, and defying the changes and chances of time,

Deep-based on the laws now unriddled, the facts
    that are fixed, the sublime

Long labour, success of our fathers, who silent,
    yet speak !

O the endless progression of thought, from the
    schools of the Greek,

And the city of scholars deep-brained, who could
    gather the gift

Of the wonder and wealth of the past, who had
    patience to sift

And to hand on the best to the new generation,
    aflash with the flame

Of the glorified Nazarene's fire, whose immaculate
    Name

Shook down the strong thrones of the Cæsars, and
    set up in place,

Self-sacrifice sweeter than life, meek might of
    invisible grace,

Then came the slow struggles of creed, the age
    of the Councils, debates,

Fierce factions, malign persecutions, betrayals,
    intolerant hates ;

Still, under the crystalised dogma, the bull of
  infallible Pope,

Dilemma, and logic of schoolmen ; the seed of
  humanity's hope

Grew in cloister and castle, cathedral and convent ;
  the effort was one :

Monk, merchant, crusader and monarch, proud lady
  and nun,

They laboured, they fought, and they loved and
  they yearned for the best,

For the something Divine yet unconquered, the
  dream that would not let them rest,

Unsatisfied still, they grasped at the future, till
  out of the East

Rang an echo ; " This earth is not wholly a
  snare of the Beast ;

The beauty that lures thee in Nature and woman,
  the simple delight

Of innocent children, of homestead, and garden,
  is good and is right ;

There is joy in the finite, the lisp of the least
  leaf may thrill thee, the hell

Of the Eremite's madness, the scourge, the
    seclusion, the ban and the cell

Are marks of vain torture, of helpless endeavour
    to break through the bond

Of flesh that imprisons, that bars thee from vision
    of wonders beyond :

But the wonder is round thee, the dust that thou
    spurnest is pregnant with truth,

The books thou contemnest of Hellas are blossoms
    of Nature and youth ;

No longer gaze mournfully over humanity blasted
    by sin,

No longer strive vainly to solve the sphinx-riddle
    by searching within,

There is earth at thy feet, there is life in the
    street, there are joys that are clean :

Go, mix with thy fellows, despise not God's
    creatures ; th' unseen and the seen

Must mingle, enlighten, correct one another—thy
    visions of love

Beyond, are not all—all that is thou must love
    that the world may improve."

Thus grew the great Age of New Learning. There
were feuds, there were fights

For freedom of conscience, for government civil,
political rights :

And the wave of progression swept forward.

Then woke with a burst

From her feudal oppression a Spirit of marvel in
men, and a thirst

For adventure and travel and knowledge of others,
impassioned delight

As of children who gaze the first time on a
glorious sight ;

They swept round the world, they ransacked the
ages, translated and taught ;

They lived hard, they worked hard, they died
hard ; they sought and they fought

For something they deemed very precious, not
above nor beneath,

But for liberty dearer than life, and for love that
is deeper than death,

Here, here, on this earth. And like Titans they
groaned with ambitious desire

To wield from the heights of Olympus the bolt of
invincible fire.

Then budded the rod of our Empire; aye, chips
of the oak

Were the sires of the sons of the West, who have
flung off the yoke ;

But one blood and one race with one speech are
we still, and a time

Draweth nigh for a closer alliance to blot out the
crime

Of that futile oppression.

And then broke in battle a terrible dawn :

'Twixt the rights of a Monarch, the wrongs of a
People, the kingdom was torn ;

Heaven guided that issue through triumph and
failure: the struggle was stern :

But the strength of the nation was solid and patient,
could suffer and learn,

Though a frost chilled the early success, and
fanatical gloom

Wrapt all the gray island: but silently under the doom

Of depression and stillness, as under the cloak of the snow

Bursts a delicate snowdrop, that tells of the promise of spring,

Waxed the weak flower of science, a modest and tentative thing,

(While the rest of the landscape lay formless and featureless, pale as a ghost):

That clung to the earth, and was slow in its growth, hardly noticed by most,

But still there it was.

        And when Winter at last had gone by,

There ran a faint tremulous shudder through Europe, a sigh

Of oppression and hatred against the oppressor, but not a soul stirr'd:

And a voice of revolt against tyranuous priestcraft which nobody heard:

In revel by moonlight with courtier and mistress the monarch sat throned:

And under the feet of the monarch the angel of
Liberty groaned:

"What are kings? what are rights? what,
religion?" the sceptic enquired:

"Mere tricks of the stronger to harass the weaker,
gross selfishness tired

And trapp'd in deceitful apparel—society's built

On a lie—back to nature and freedom," they
cried: "let the guilt

Be avenged of their sons and their fathers: come,
let us restore

The reign of the people primæval."

Then rose with a roar,

As of beasts of the forest when twilight is falling,
a nation enraged,

And wreak'd their red fury in wreckage and blood
till their wrath was assuaged;

Till out of their ranks climbed a despot, remorselessly strong,

A man of the people, who led them to glory, and
Europe ere long

Lay flat at his feet. But he fell at the last, and
his deeds were as dust

That reddens a terrible sunset: the fame of his
reign and his lust

As the flare of a portent that flashes and fades
from the sky:

But the dream of democracy widened.

And science arose,

And strode through the dark in the shape of a
giant, a giant that throws

The shadow of dread upon all that he passes: the
woods quake with fear:

At the sound of his footstep, the ring of his
hammer, the hills disappear;

He measures and mutters, the seas cannot check
his imperious stride:

He blows his great horn through the storm: as
he plunges his steel in the tide,

Waves leap to obey him, no darkness benights him,
he watches in sleep :

The roll of the ocean he changes to light as he
    lolls on the deep,

While all the huge weight of his mail the mad
    waters must keep,

Though they curl their white lips, hiss and heave
    in his wake, they must toil at command,—

Soon became the great gests of this giant a power
    in the land;

For his eyes were so clear he could tell what the
    stars were composed of, and note

All those little black minims that lurk in man's body
    to hurt him, and float

Else unseen, in the air; and his ear was so keen
    that no sound could escape,

But words that were murmured at Cairo he caught
    at the Cape;

But strangest of all were the tales that he told;
    for like Zadig the sage,

The hound and the horse that he never had seen,
    he described: and the age

Of the earth, and the various races of men, what
    they saw, what they prized,

Ere Memphis was raised from the dust, or the tombs of the Pharoahs devised:

And he spake with authority too of men's faith and men's fears;

"Aye, what were their creeds and their shibboleths now in the ocean of years!

He had made all religion a science, could trace how belief had evolved

Through totem and fetich and ancestor-worship:— the question was solved:

And man's mind was a delicate web of gray matter, priest-figment the soul;

His will but the ultimate strongest sensation that governs the whole:

His freedom a farce, his crime a disease, and his faith a fine folly."

So spake the dread giant, and straightway on all fell profound melancholy.

Behold, I will sing of myself, for myself am a part of the whole,

John Self, the waif of the hopes of his age with the chant in his soul:

For a nation brought me to birth, 'tis futile for
them to disown;

For I have not sprung like a palm in the desert,
self-sown and alone,

But the desolate Past with long sighing and labour,
and passionate fire,

As he yearn'd for his shadowy Psyche, the Future,
his unseen desire,

Begat me: behold me, believe me, I am what
I am,

With the frame of my father who sleeps with his
fathers, but eyes lit with flame

Of the lady my mother, the deathless, the dauntless,
half-veiled and half-seen,

And I feel that she will not deceive or disgrace
me, my mother, my queen.

For oft, when the folds of the twilight have fallen
and covered the land,

In the fields I have wandered and pondered and
felt for her hand,

For the stately white hand of the lady my mother,
when roses are blowing;

And raptured with glory of summer and gloaming moved on without knowing,

Till stealthily out of the scent and the mist and the gloom of the wood,

In place of her hand, there has fallen a kiss on my lips, and a mood

Of clairvoyance, ineffable insight, and buoyant delight ;

And I know that the soul shall strive onward till reason and love shall unite :

Till passion and purity blend, and the "ought" and the " is " be as one,

Till love shall no longer be wild, nor knowledge wax sterile alone,

Till the heart shall not shrink from the head, nor the head be betrayed by the heart;

When the lion and lamb shall lie down together, religion with art,

And the weanèd child shall place his hand on the cocatrice-den,

Aye, faith shall not swerve from science, nor science be faithless then.

The ways of the world without shall not war with
the world within,

Nor the fruit of the tree of knowledge be plucked
from the boughs of sin,

The apple of love shall not waste in the mouth to
the dust of remorse,

Nor the face of a thousand ships bear the freight
of a nation's curse.

Our girls and our boys will be brought up together,
no longer divorced,

United in wiser reliance on nature, not fettered,
not forced ;

The mind of the girl must be braced by the boy's;
no more shall inanity

Strangle the growth of her best, or swallow her
talents in vanity;

The boy will be touched by the grace of the
maiden, and sweetened in soul,

Till from knowledge of either arise something
better than knowledge—control.

The poet's heart shall not ache for the ways and
the days of the dead,

For the present shall thrill and exalt him when
knowledge and love have wed,

No more shall his bosom heave like a salt and a
homeless sea

Plunging in desolate search of the shores of
eternity,

Nor shatter in cynical spray 'gainst the floes of the
world's cold face,

Nor batten and waste on the drift of the wash of
the commonplace :

No, no, O receive me, believe me. take back, 'tis
thine own,

This faith in my soul, of the future prophetic : leap,
leap to thy throne,

Reign there ! thou art king in the realm of thy
splendour, no more thou art dust,

'Tis faith that must crown thee triumphant in effort :
the ultimate trust

That dies unrewarded, that marks the divergence of
manhood from beast :

And this in its essence may be the possession of
greatest and least.

I sing not of heroes, for all flesh is goodly, alike
 in the main ;

I claim no advantage of birth or possession, I
 share what I gain ;

I stand with my fellows, I need them : together
 we thrive or we fall,

The sin and the sorrow of one is the sorrow and
 sin of us all :

Society holds us and folds us in fetters far firmer
 than brass,

'Tis as drops of the ocean, as leaves of the oak
 tree, as green blades of grass ;

'Tis the pageant of millions that moves us to
 marvel, the measureless sweep

Of the fields of the harvest, the gloom of the
 forest, the roar of the deep,

And my spirit in rapture flings forth a proud pæan,
 caresses the whole ;

We lend to each other our best and our bravest
 —I give you my soul—

Nay, 'tis not my soul, 'tis the soul of a nation
 that beats in this song ;

For myself. I am nothing, I rank with the file, I
am one with the throng.

O Father almighty, Thou wilt not deceive us, Thou
wilt not protract

The night of our sorrow, the dream of our doubting,
the faith which we lacked,

For now through the mouth of this people and all
men by me thou art praised.

O mother immortal, dear earth, thy dark atoms of
matter are raised,

Mysterious, are raised in the scale of our knowledge :
we bow, and we trust.

O mother protean, immortal, abiding, that weavest
the dust

To shapes of full splendour through seasons of
wonder, maturity, rest ;

That buildest and breakest, that turnest and shakest
the mould in thy palm,

As of old thou wilt feed us and shepherd thy
chosen and shield them from harm.

Round these brows at my birth 'twas a bough of
green olive, of olive, not yew,

Thou didst twine as a sign of peace of the soul
thou would'st grant, not to few,

But to all who would walk in the ways of thy
wisdom and help thine increase:

And this promise to those who will follow and
serve thee—thy palm and thy peace.

SONG OF THE WANDERER'S RETURN

1

Hell, pack your fading fires,

Stars, freeze your worst:

I'll quench my deep desires,

I'll see my lady first.

I come, I come.

2

From rugged Russian floes,

Icefields and bears,

When scarlet dawn arose

Love heard my prayers.

I come, I come.

3

By Ganges' floating lamp,
  Crocodiles cry :
Jungle and veldt and swamp,
  World-wanderer I :
        I come, I come.

4

Cast me your horoscope,
  Stars overhead ;
Lighter than antelope.
  Hark, 'tis her tread,
        She comes, she comes.

5

Thou art a woman.
  I am a man :
Love, love is human,
  Life is a span.
        I come, I come.

6.

Tease me no more, ye Fates,

   Under this dome!

Breathless before your gates.

           I come, I come.

Love, take me home!

LOVE'S CONQUEST

1

Here let the billowy tempest overtake us

    Of love, of love;

Here let his arrowy lightnings rend and shake us,

    Time will approve;

Heaven comes not closer than a woman's heart,

Or none, or all, I crave! O love me not in part.

2

I am no false half-hearted wayward lover,

    The passion comes:

I plunge, my foot not deigning to recover,

    I love but once;

God-like should be the wooing lover's strength!

O let me anchor on this happy isle at length.

3

Nay! tell me not to move mine eyes away,

            Dread not their fire :

Lust, sloth, and envy now have had their day,

            Gazing, expire :

It is thy cleansing soul I hunger for,

It is the God in thee I yield to and adore.

4

Lift up these gates immortal, let me wonder,

            Oh! have I won?

Mine, wholly mine, till life's stout bark go under,

            The voyage done :

Lightnings may cease,—let joy descend in tears,

And this sweet rain make rich the hope of future
years.

A FALLING STAR

1

Did sleep refuse your gentle eyes

Last night, and did you sit awhile

While moonlight filled the summer skies;

And watching with a wistful smile

Still muse about that shooting star

You saw, while we were walking home;

When fearful of hard days to come,

You gazed, and wondered what we are!

2

And fragrant memories at my heart,

Like violets drenched in April dew

Revived :—while hope, the nobler part

Of life, began to thrill anew;

Sweet voices hailed me from the grave,

Far o'er the sea, where shadows shroud

Death's garden, and sheer cliffs of cloud

Blot out the dead whose names we save.

3

We children in life's pilgrimage,

What can we know? a pious guess;

But Eden-tones and sacred page

Hint something deeper than success :

Let us be clear :   " We do not know,"

So falls that star ; and then perchance

From honest night of ignorance

A dawn of deeper truth may flow.

4

Life's not for victory or prize,

But effort only, as it seems ;

The will, the work, the enterprise.

And sunny days for sowing dreams ;

We sow, we reap; lovers and friends;

And what remains of cherished hours?

Only a knot of faded flowers,

And memory—so, so it ends.

5.

One royal moment on his throne

Love sits triumphant over death,

Calls the wide universe his own,

And lives an æon in a breath :

He mingles, mid that short delight,

With music borne from worlds afar :

Then, like an inharmonious star,

Swerves : and shoots headlong down the night.

6

We are but wanderers. Let us stand,

Though rains wash bare life's ruined pride,

And ocean swallow sea and land,

Though not a soul stand by our side,

Unbribed, unsuccoured, undismayed,

Still let us stand and conquer;—aye,

The red rose withers on its stem.

What is life's final diadem?

Death—love's last utterance—a sigh.

A HARMLESS DITTY

At dusk we took our walk abroad,

        O fie !   O fie !

I stole a kiss along the road :

        Tra la la, tra la le.

She blushed and would not look at me,

        O fie !   O fie !

And so I made the kisses three :

        Tra la la, tra la le.

And no one came along the lane,

        O fie !   O fie !

She gave me one o' them back again :

        Tra la la, tra la le.

Like me may every lover thrive,

        O fie !   O fie !

I feel quite glad to be alive :

        Tra la la, tra la le.

ALONE!

1

Firm of purpose, God-reliant,

Parted and alone I sit:

Still the spirit is defiant,

Bleed on heart—what of it?

2

Doubtless love's a heaven-sent blessing,

Life's one peerless aloe-bud,

Still not given us for possessing,

What comes next?—Solitude.

LULLABY

1

O to fling down this weary head
'Mong valleys where they never reap:
A pillow of poppies for my bed,
And dream-dews from the Latmian steep;
 Thy brown wings hover,
 Cover, O cover,
And shield me with thy pinion, sleep!

2

Sing smoother measures than the airs
That blow round Lesbos, famous isle,
Drop down, and take me unawares,
To roam and roam thy realm awhile;
 Till night be over,
 And dawn uncover
My dreaming eyelids with a smile.

LOVE'S PATIENCE

1

Can the life be worth the living

That locks up the human heart?

Can the love be worth the giving

That surrenders but in part?

Life should be a generous giver

Full of bounty and increase :

Love, a slow, majestic river

Deepening through a land of peace

2

Can a man be worth the waiting,

If he dare not cope with fate?

Can a maid be worth the mating,

If too fickle-frail to wait?

So, my heart, I bend and kiss you,

Like a lover true and brave,

Though faith only see the issue,

Love will last beyond the grave.

LOVER AND MORALIST

LOVER :   Let sorrow come, I'll not regret.

MORALIST :   Though love should wither with the
             leaf ?

LOVER :   It was in summer that we met.

MORALIST :   Love's summer days are hot and brief.

LOVER :   The heart-shaped cherry on the bough
             Allured the glossy starling's beak :

MORALIST :   Fit emblem how a lover's vow
             Can win and waste a blushing cheek.

2

LOVER : Red breathless clouds streamed up the
East,

And hail'd the sun-god from afar :

The thrill Earth felt within her breast,

A thrush sang to the dying star ;

Hark ! hark ! the lark's auroral cry

That light as wine leapt in our veins :

" All other raptures cannot buy

The least of love's immortal pains."

THE COST OF VICTORY

1

Profounder peace my soul invades
    Than, after battle's blood and strain,
Lulls the broad field, when evening shades
    The silent faces of the slain.

2

There, hopes like stricken heroes lie
    Foe-facing, with their eyes aghast ;
Joys bivouaced 'neath the open sky :
    O joys ! too proud, too young to last !

3

Alone, I pass across the field
    By moonlight, 'neath the tranquil trees :
God never meant the right to yield,
    'Twas worth the loss to gain this peace.

4

The splash of blood, charge and recnarge,

The whirl and scream of shell and shot,

A man must meet: would he enlarge

The kingdom native to his lot.

A ghostly combat 'twas, meseems

By far the fiercest fight of all:

These sighing hopes and splintered dreams

Shall claim most solemn burial.

6

With calm I count the fearful cost,

And inwardly exult; although

I ne'er shall head a braver host,

Nor gaze upon a fairer show.

LONELY LOVE

1

And if I love thee, what is that to thee !
Will not the sunflower bow toward the sun ?
What's one pale star when morning has begun,
And who in youth remembers memory ?

2

We met as friends, as friends we part again :
Go and be happy, break another heart !
Thou soon wilt learn to play that higher part,
And pride will teach me how to smother pain.

3

Ah me, I toil, I ache to comprehend :
O moon and sea, O stars and miles of sand
Where once we used to wander, hand in hand.
Nor ever wonder how it all would end ?

4

O wild-wood walks ! O fire of youth's ambition !

Alone with thee along the moon-lit corn.

That moon has fled, how bleak the fields stand
shorn !

And cold neglect the meed of woman's mission.

5

Nay, but the heart is such a tender plant,

So sensitive to sunshine and to rain :

A gust will make that blossom shut again,

Nor future music as of old enchant.

6

Why teach me love if but to leave me thus,

That melody's too sad to sing alone :

Love aches to sit upon a single throne,

Her unshared honours how monotonous !

7

To wait while beauty withers silently,

Me, me, thy spring-tide's sweetheart left alone :

O home which once I thought to call mine own,

O phantom faces I shall never see !

AN AUTUMN SONG

1

What is this pang that strikes across my heart ?

A silent flush

On field and bush

No wild wood-thrush doth waken.

2

What are these tears that tremble down my cheek ?

Must I alone

Live on to mourn

My loved ones flown, or taken ?

3

What is this splendour streams across my soul ?

Fight the good fight.

We shall unite

When earth lies quite forsaken.

THE SAND-FLOWER

Where ocean breaks on either hand

Along a bleak and sterile shore,

Where tongues of surf lick up the sand,

Amid the wreckage and the roar.

Where heaps of blackened seaweed lie

Mid matted drift of various tides,

Which, as the refluent wave subsides,

Bevel the blue bald pebbles, I

Found this sweet blossom blowing.

2

There was no other verdure near,

Only the straggling thistle crawled,

And some few bents of salt bleached grass

Told to the wanderer who might pass

Of earth's last edge: where one might hear

The stormy seagull as he called.

And watch the full tide flowing.

3

The central strength of all we see

Has not this flower's immaculacy,

Yon seagull poised on outstretched wings

Still wants the scent this blossom flings;

The huffling sea-wind sweeps and blows;

This never argues,—but it grows,

And praises God in growing.

4

Sweet flower! how keen was my surprise,

And not untouched by earnest shame,

To note you there with eager eyes,

And yet to never know your name!

By what mute gift, what subtle spell,

Could you transform with chymic power
Mere sandy waste and salt sea-swell,
Into this lovely lilac flower
I press within my bosom?

5

And yet I need not marvel: for
In crowded cities far from view,
Pure souls fast locked by love's stern law,
Whose names not e'en the wisest knew,
Have lived; and by some wondrous grace,
Some art of sweeter alchemy,
Some charm of rarest charity,
Have touched to life the commonplace,
And bade the desert blossom.

THE METAPHYSICIAN

1

The lonely scholar shut his book,
   And rose and stirr'd his dying fire.
Still standing, he began to look
   And watch the winter-day expire:
And as he saw the vapours roll
   Across the meadows far away,
Mesmeric twilight brimmed his soul,
   And filmed his eyes with ecstasy.

2

Through his mist-clouded window pane,
   The tracery of twigs and boughs,
The leafless hedges rank with rain,
   Even the sheep-flocks and the cows

Seemed strangely still.—"Ah me," he cried,

"Is the world really what it seems,

Or are we cheated and belied

By incommunicable dreams?

3

"For now I feel so wierdly dull,

So plunged in doubts I cannot prove,

Lethargic and insensible

To this tough world in which we move,

That almost I am prone to say,

Gazing o'er yon grey waste of mist,

That th' ego is refined away

Sometimes, and ceases to exist.

4

"Why else this drear-eyed dreamy gaze

Over the fields at twilight tide,

If this life be not but a phase

Of some far larger life; allied,

Yet torn from which, th' atomic frame

　Obeys the spirit's plangent stress,

And deadens, while the yearning flame

　Flies forth into the wilderness.

5

" For all the fossil-forms that print

　Past strata of the growth of man,

Whatever mind or memory hint,

　I piece together as I can,

If haply—ah! but who can know,

　What single brain can grasp the whole?

Where is the science that can show

　The structure of the human soul?"

THE HEIGHTS OF WINDER

1

Red chanticleer's loud clarion calls,

  And chides the mists, and bids them pass:

Alike on loose unmorticed walls,

  On slanting roof, and sparkling grass,

Frost, like a million grains of spelt,

Glints, as the rolling vapours melt.

2

O valley of a thousand rills

  That falling, feed the dark main river;

O ring of proud and royal hills

  That stand consolidate for ever

'Twas ye, 'twas ye who rear'd my youth,

Who gave me strength and taught me truth.

3

These sun-smit summits, unperplexed

    By clouds blown crossways o'er the skies,

Fill me, by many a fancy vexed,

    With silent hope and deep surmise :

Clouds too may loiter round the base,

But splendour fills the mountain's face.

4

Yon mountain doth not mock its star,

    Nor envy swell the lesser hills,

Content they stand for what they are,

    And laugh through all their lyric rills:

These steep'd my mind, or great or less,

    In something sweeter than success.

5

Something that cannot be o'erthrown,

    Methinks, this mountain doth express ;

A conscious might that stands alone,

K

A majesty, a gentleness,

Which bids me follow what is best,

    Unchecked:—and leave to God the rest.

6

There is a Voice speaks in the air

    Of worlds that lie as yet unproved:

A Presence o'er me everywhere,

    Which will not argue but is loved:

A Message, howsoever sent,

    Which is its own best argument.

THE TWILIGHT STAR

1

Lone lamp of twilight, vestal star so distant,

   Sole sentinal ere thy myriad sisters glow,

Star of the east, eve after eve persistent,

   Marking the spot whence dawn will surely flow:

2

Storms blow, and blot thee out from man's divining,

   Thou'rt lost, thou'rt gone, the sore faint-hearted say;

And yet full well I know thou still art shining,

   It is the clouds, the clouds, which pass away.

3

O twilight star, symbol of light more tender,

   Star of the soul, guide of distempered youth ;

In sovereign faith I yield complete surrender,

   And henceforth follow in the track of truth.

4

Thou, round thine orbit, journeyest, never swerving

From that fixed course in which the planets move:

O soul, swerve not from that great law of serving

By which thy being mounts through endless love.

OFT IN ELYSIAN RAPTURE

1

Oft in Elysian rapture have I wandered
   O'er dell and down, through glen and grove,
Where'er my footsteps led me, I have pondered
   The royal song, the perfect love.

2

Alas! what lips of clay can ever sing us
   The song of songs, the royal chant?
And who of mortals breatheth that can bring us
   The love of loves, the love we want?

GOOD-NIGHT—NOT GOOD-BYE

I

There is a word that wrings the heart,

And oh! too soon it must be spoken,

It comes when those who meet must part,

When scenes will change, and ties are broken.

Broken ?

No, no,

Not so,

There still will be some tie.

2

Kind hearts are not too far away,

Some token of good-will to send us,

Though some will go, and some must stay,

Still as of old may God defend us ;

Good-bye ?

No, no,

Not so,

Good-night—ah! not good-bye!

A MAGIC FIELD

1

A field, a field, down in the west,
Green, open to the sun and air :
A gust of love, a throbbing breast,
I could not cross it but in prayer.

2

For ever on that plot of ground
Some angel touched away my tears,
And heavenly echoes rang around
The narrow arches of mine ears.

3

They sang me songs of anguish old,
Mute loves, and measures of delight :
I trod the fabled fleece of gold
In mail of more than human might.

4

For hate grew distant as a dream,
And sorrow shed a subtle bliss ;
Deep in my breast there swam a beam
Of faith and melting tenderness.

5

The dead, the living, e'en as one,
Seemed singing through the twilight-air :
Time withered with the rolling sun,
And solace crowned the brows of care.

6

I paused and stretched mine arms abroad,
And then wrote swiftly with my pen :
" He who has felt the peace of God
Can work without the praise of men."

SEHNSUCHT

1

Fresh, fresh as a rose is the face of the Earth,

Immortal, abiding, Protean,

The death of a shower is the dew of the birth

Of a song-bird's imperious pæan.

2

But unknown, unexplored is the core of the Earth,

Too abysmal for human discerning :

Though her surface be flattered with seasons of mirth,

Her breast is remorselessly burning.

3

But fairest of all is the rose of the Earth,

Man—man—Nature's prodigal giant :

The death of a dream is to him but the birth

Of resolve, philosophic, defiant.

4

But unplumbed is man's mystery still, though the worth

Of his years be consumed in the learning;

Like the central sad fires of his mother, the Earth:

His bosom is wasted with yearning.

A PAGAN CHORALE

Vex not thy soul with dread of death's accruing,
  Hush! hush all sorrows in forgetfulness;
Weep not in dreams, the past is past pursuing,
  The future but a vain elusive guess;
Let poppy twine thy tares, when the last embers
  Of life's gray fires drop on the cold hearth-stone:
Sleep! and dismiss the spirit that remembers
  All that thy days have done or left undone.

Come heavenly sleep, sink gently on his eyelids,
  O Hermes! touch his forehead with thy wand,
And guide him kindly when the last low sigh bids
  Thy presence waft him to a world beyond.

A BOY'S DAY-DREAM

All day he sat beside the pond,

And none rebuked ; for none could guess

The boy's retreat : no careless feet

Broke in upon his solitude ;

The cuckoo and the wilderness

Were the grand masons of his mood ;

With bricks of water, and airy mortar,

He built a turret and gazed beyond.

2

A thousand spirits he had, that gleam

Or creep or swim or live by the chase :

And magic spells from mystic wells

That hold in leash the skipping fays ;

Such made obeisance to his grace,

And fast as ants in Autumn days,

With song and sod, with trowel and hod,

They reared the battlement of dream.

3

A parapet of delicate make

With loop-holes cleft at intervals

Crowned the great tower ; and here a bower

A misty staircase led unto :

And from the summit a fountain falls

Of rainbow bubbles and drizzling dew :

And over the fountain, vista of mountain,

Blue sky, and beauty—his thirst to slake.

4

The boy gazed up, his large gray eyes

Absorbed in speculation : Lo--

Sudden there stood upon the flood

A naked figure, athletic, slim,

Flushed with the glory of love aglow

For a whiter phantom, that shadowed dim,

Beyond the fountain, beyond the mountain ;

Half seen, half veiled behind the skies.

5

The fountain figure stretched his arms,

Crying aloud : " My heart will break !—

If thou art real, O white ideal,

Stoop down and kiss me lest I die ;

Stoop and caress."—He seemed to wake

A million echoes with his cry :

And fairy fountain, figure and mountain

And tower collapsed in loud alarms.

TO A YOUNG POET

1

A voice! a voice! do you not hear it ringing

 O'er fen and fold?

A poet's voice, do you not hear him singing

 The new, and old?

2

I saw him lying, laughing in the clover,

 Though none was near;

The meadows cry'd: "Welcome! the world's true
lover

 Is here, is here."

3

All down the green glade late and early roaming,

 In leafy grove,

I heard him softly singing: in the gloaming

 He sang of love

SIR HUMPHREY GILBERT'S LAST VOYAGE

"Sail on my bark, my bark sail on,

The moon is fled, the stars are gone."

>The lightnings quiver,

>The tempest shrieks:

>The yard-arms shiver,

>The cordage creaks.

"Furl sail, batter down the hatches:"

"Master, the hurricane catches us,

Master, the hurricane snatches us!"

"Sail on my bark, my bark sail on,

Until the storm be overblown:

Little I reck of wrack or rent,

The five bells chime, the night is spent."

>"A shout, a shout,

>Put about, put about,

>A sailor overboard."

" Nay, leave him to the Lord,

For ship and soul on sea or land

Are close to God's almighty hand :

Sail on my bark, my bark sail on,

The moon is dead, the stars have flown ;

When the great storm of storms is past,

Man's destiny will clear at last."

> His strength is weak,
>
> His currents crossed ;
>
> " A leak, a leak,
>
> We're lost, we're lost ! "

" Master, the stern crushes in on us,

Master, the sea rushes in on us,

> Lost, lost, all lost ! "

" Lost,—nay not lost, the haven's won,

Sink, sink, my bark, thy course is done,

For ship and soul on sea or land

Are close to God's almighty hand."

L

NATURE'S ETHICS

1

And when my brain is overwrought

With toil or solitary thought,

When all my fevered pulses beat,

And this flesh-prison throbs and thrills,

I sit beside the window-seat

Where oft I sat in boyhood's days,

And through the frost-bound silence, gaze

Upon the white majestic hills.

2

So meek, so stern, so wondrous still

They stand: they fortify my will

With strength the world knows nothing of;

With haughty silence to endure,

And with sincerity, to prove

That Nature's work knows no regrets,

She never falters or forgets,

Her paths are plain, her purpose sure.

3

Behind man's riot and life's folly,

Life's failure and man's melancholy,

Broods the great destiny, the plan

Slowly unfolded hour by hour

In Nature, and the soul of man ;

This is not changed, nor disappears,

But rules the rolling of the spheres,

And whispers through the frailest flower.

THE POPLARS

1

Not a voice, not a sound of the step of men,

 The shadowy kine on the uplands lie:

Not a bird is heard, not a stir from the glen,

 But only the slender poplars sigh.

2

On the hard white road glints the cusp of the moon,

 The land is cool'd with the wind's caress:

There is joy on all of the choral June,

 And the poplars utter their happiness.

3

For summer speaks to the world once more,

 Her music moves on the wings of the breeze,

O Love! thou art queen, from the sap and the core

 To the tips of the musical poplar-trees.

4

O mystical love! O magic unsung,

That thy sorceress-spirit in secrecy weaves!

Ah! where among men is the silver-sweet tongue

To sing us the song of the poplar-leaves?

(THE SONG)

(1)

Then fly with me; my love, with me:

June, June is ours, I love, I yearn :

A land of flowers, and reverie,

The poplars lisp love's low nocturn.

(2)

Ah! it must ever come to this,

When love and youth and summer meet:

To wake a smile, to win a kiss,

I'd cast an empire at thy feet.

(3)

Where thou art, the immortals are,

To breathe thy sweet Elysian breath

Would make a glow-worm grow a star,

And teach a dastard scorn of death.

(4)

Thy tones are like that solemn lyre

The stress of Nature speaketh through,

Thine eyes are moons of mellow fire,

Thy mouth a moss-rose moist with dew.

(5)

O come with me ; my love, with me :

June, June will die, I sigh, I yearn ;

Ope to the night's fond witchery,

My lily of the golden urn.

(6)

Steep me with nectar of thy mind,

    Love's aromatic chalice spill:

No third is here: only a wind

    Keeps tryst upon the moon-lit hill.

(7)

O earth, O earth, how strange thou art,

    How new-created all that is;

When love, fore-gathering at the heart,

    First trembles in a mutual kiss.

DOWN STREAM

Who would not drift on such a stream

    At such an hour, alone with thee,

Together, you and I, Marie,

    Who would not drift, who would not dream?

A while ago the full sun sank,

    And twilight gathered in the trees,

The slender reeds on either bank,

    With summer piped: "Say, who are these

That, dropping down an odorous wind,

    Slide smoothly past my rushy coves?"

"We leave a world of tears behind

    In search of secret treasure-troves:"

The swimming lilies softly sighed:

    "'Tis but a lover and his bride."

2

"We are alone. Still, as of old,

  To hear thy voice above the flood,

Ten times ten thousand strings of gold,

  Dear Marie, throb and thrill my blood.

But thou art as a faultless flower

  That sheds still perfume on the air.

What time the bee from manna-bower

  Wings forth, and searches everywhere :

And still the slim white throated flower

  Utters no sound, divinely dumb,

She rests on Nature's secret power.

  She knows the bee is sure to come :

So thou, sweet mistress, hast the art

  Of silence to enchant the heart

3

"I've watched the goldfinch in the mead

  With fluttered palpitating wings

Poised close above the thistle-seed :

And still he hovers, still she swings,

And still the winds, in captious play,

Her crest incline, his feathers puff,

Where'er he turns, she bends away;

And every slip and shy rebuff

But makes his hunger keener felt;

So, when I bow, and fain would press

My lips to hers, and fondly melt

In speech no language can express,

She moves, and I, poor fool, must miss

The music of my lady's kiss.

4

" How did my love begin ?—a gleam

From paradise that shot, and spread

Within my soul : a heavenly beam

Pulsing in waves of joy and dread :

Ah ! bid this deep majestic stream

Flow back, and seek his fountain-head.

We met : for better or for worse :

For worse ? Ah ! no, it cannot be,

Love needs must take its own sweet course

    In light and shadow to the sea;

But ask not love's immortal source.

5

"Adown the maiden mountain-beck

    I've watched the eddies wreathe and swirl,

And scented bells of heather speck

    The dimpled flood : so coil and curl

The ringlets round thy slender neck,

    While drifts of fancy flush and fleck

The claustral cheek, the gates of pearl.

6

" Look up, Marie, this is our tryst :

    Away, away o'er stream and glen,

Ringed round and cloaked in cloud and mist,

Moves the great world of other men:

O let me be thy world alone,

As thou art mine, and only mine,

My heart shall be thy single throne,

Sole home, thy soul, so I am thine."

7

"O hold me and fold me belovèd,

I love thee:

If still thou must doubt me, then try me,

Then prove me:

O love, the subduer, will change not

With fashion,

Say, which is the truer, the world or

My passion:

As twilight with moonlight when daylight

Is over,

So eyesight wakes soul-sight in maiden

And lover;

Let fortune caress thee; sin, sorrow

Oppress me:

Still, still must I follow and worship

And bless thee:

O silent, still doubting! then test me

And prove me:

But, hold me and fold me, belovèd,

I love thee."

8

" Aye, and thou love me, as thou art,

So fresh and pure, so proud and fair,

And if thou give me all thine heart

This moment as thou liest there,

Thou of thy single self shalt prove,

Men grow immortal when they love.

9

" The earth will crumble like the past,

Dead are the dreams of long ago,

How little may the present last !

 'Tis come and gone ere one can know :

A glance, a gleam, a moment's quiver

 Of moonlight on a flowing river.

10

" And shall this gaudy world mislead

 The man who sighs for sober rest ?

Ambition, Fortune, fame ?—indeed

 I find them all upon thy breast,

And in sincere simplicity

 Utterly give myself to thee.

11

" Death's finger cannot touch the bough

 That hangs in love's celestial bower ;

Love's life is an immortal now,

 A present never-dying hour.

When love and time meet ; in their kiss,

 Eternity is all that is."

OCTOBER—GOOD-BYE

I

The small brown brook swirls rapidly,

And gathered are the barley-sheaves :

Amid a fall of fading leaves

Our footsteps meet to say good-bye !

2

Come, let us stand where the road runs nigh

This side the heavy whitewashed gate,

Where wet square ricks stand desolate,

There let us wish and kiss good-bye !

3

The loose-leaf'd willows lean and sigh

Along the field where the brown brook flows,

How soon the day draws to its close !

How soon 'tis time to say good-bye !

4

Let us be resolute, and try

To find some utterance for relief;

Nor wrapt in mist of mournful grief,

Wait, dumb like cattle—you and I !

5

Loitering alone here, you and I

Can find no fond exchange of words:

We hang as silent as the birds,

It is so sad to say good-bye !

6

Needs must, from this low-weeping sky

I chase your twittering swallow south ;

One last sweet silence, mouth to mouth :

Friends once, friends ever ! Love, good-bye !

AUTUMN TOUCHES

1

Now drops the fir-cone from the fir,

Ripe acorns patter through the oaks,

And half dismantled stands the wood,

The blue jay screams, the bull-frog croaks :

Safe garnered is the golden corn,

And glossy starlings boldly dash

And strip the scarlet mountain-ash.

The red may-berry hangs forlorn.

2

Where late stream'd tongues of scented bloom

Black hang the laburnum's shrivell'd pods,

The elm-tree sheds her small firm leaves,

The slim mast-poplar, naked, nods :

M

The orchard stands despoiled of fruit,

And barren boughs begin to show

Thick clumps of sage-green mistletoe,

While all the meads are moist and mute

3

The filbert slips its russet sheath.

And walnut boughs are beaten bare,

A white mist crawls from vale to vale,

And shrewdly bites the evening air,

Tired flocks at twilight steal to fold ;

With burrowing mole the soil is loose,

And now the plough-boy sets his noose,

And earth-worms cast the mounded mould.

4

Dimpled with bent and willow-leaf,

O'er bedded reeds the shallow stream,

'Twixt tiny isle and shelving bank

Where dace in summer bask and gleam,

Runs and will run, till Boreas blow

His boisterous clarion through the gloom.

And cloak his course and seal his doom

With thickening frost and furious snow.

5

Cold hangs the nest beneath the thatch

Where late the circling swallow hung,

Weak linnets cloud the homestead ricks,

The sparrow pecks the farmyard dung ;

Now hums the farmer's threshing-wheel,

And village children with their books

Peep in to watch the tossing stooks,

Then scamper away to mid-day meal.

6

The cub-fox knows his secret lair.

The hedgehog rolls himself to rest.

The cold snake curls beneath the leaves,

The mouse has weaved her winter nest,

Amid the thicket chirps the wren

And brusquely flits from twig to twig,

Dumb is the shrill high-elbowed grig,

The hare creeps down the marshy fen.

7

Thus all things, after their own kind,

Serve and preserve, bloom and decay:

Shall man alone, gifted with mind,

Swerve from his own appointed way?

Because of knowledge shall he fail,

Or mazed in larger ignorance,

Neglect the will, bow down to chance,

And let the cruder form prevail?

8

For each has some peculiar gift,

His bounden duty to perform:

O Earth! and can a man not lift

That which is loosened by a worm!

Shall Nature stretch an arm to save

Her meaner creatures, teach them how

To toil and thrive : yet let man go,

Mocked with half-knowledge, to the grave?

No! wider knowledge needs must print

A fuller faith upon the heart :

As hidden ways of Nature hint

Deep touches of diviner art :

'Tis good to grasp the facts of time

And search the secrets of the dust,

If but to trace how greed and lust

Expand by law, and learn to climb.

10

But shall mankind drop back and serve

The beggarly elements whence he rose,

Deny the soul, because he knows

This frame, too well, of flesh and nerve

Shall he malign his long ascent,

And let despair or passion sway:

Nor bid the loftier spirit play

On this self-conscious instrument ?

II

No, no! For though man's ancient pride

Stand stript, and autumn skies be dull;

I will not sigh as once I sighed,

As once I wept, I will not weep:

Dead forms and faces beautiful

Still gather at the wells of sleep:

Wistful, but not disconsolate

I watch the leaves drop. Rest! tired earth!

In thy decay a better birth

Quickens, and I will love and wait.

MEDIOCRITY ANSWERED

He drifts and dies who has no aim,
Tost to and fro on buffeting seas:
Better to chase the pinioned flame
Of selfish purpose, better shame
With strength—than sink in sapless ease.

2

But better far, who with shut ears
Faces his moody thoughts alone;
Few hopes survive, but fewer fears
Confuse him as the end appears,
He looks ahead without a groan.

3

We have one life, but one to spend.
How shall we use the precious loan?
Dawn is our slave, the noon a friend,
Sunset may stay: but at the end
The soul must judge the soul alone.

4

Wilt keep the same our fathers had,
Treasure the buried talent?—but
Read the old page of Nature, shut
The book without a note to add,
And plod tradition's crudded rut?

5

"Ah! but I have no worthy gift,
No genius, learning, eloquence,
I am not strong, I am not swift,
I have not power enough to lift
This weight of conscious impotence.

6

"If I had only half your might,

Your courage, your unswerving will,

I'd dare defiance, in the fight

My sword should aid the cause of right:—

But now my life is like a mill

7

" That slowly moves its measured round,

Monotonously confident ;

The stream, alas, is not profound,

The average weight of grain is ground ;

Such was the wheel's predestined bent."

8

"Can then life's mill no freedom have ?—

What stream so hidd'n but stars will steal

And glimmer somewhere on the wave :

E'en if the wheel be but a slave,

Whence comes the stream that feeds the wheel ?

9

"What seems so now confined and slow

Far up the mountain-height outbroke

With godlike energy, aye, we know

Which way the element will flow,

When it has passed beyond the yoke.

10

"Why weigh the worth of small and great?

Water's the same the whole world through,

The deepest seas plunge desolate,

And heaven itself, in spite of fate,

Can gather in one drop of dew."

LINE BROTHERS, PRINTERS, CLACTON-ON-SEA.

BUSTER AND BABY JIM.

BY THE AUTHOR OF
"THE BLUE FLAG," ETC.

"WITH GOD ALL THINGS ARE POSSIBLE."

PUBLISHED BY THE
AMERICAN TRACT SOCIETY,
150 NASSAU-STREET, NEW YORK.

CONTENTS.

CHAPTER X.

CHAPTER XI.

CHAPTER XII.

CHAPTER XIII.

BUSTER AND BABY JIM.

CHAPTER I.

THE BROTHERS.

THERE is a sunny street-corner in one of our cities, which was once the favorite lounging-place for the idle boys of all that neighborhood. In fair weather or foul, a knot of little fellows was sure to be collected there, buzzing away like bees, if they were not gathering honey. They talked and laughed and cracked their jokes, and seemed in truth a "merrie companie;" yet when the careful mothers who lived hard by sent out their sons on errands, they were sure to say, "Don't stop at the corner," or, "Go round the other way, so that you need not pass that corner."

It was not that the group of boys of which we have spoken could not boast some well-dressed lads among them, that they were condemned; no, it was not on account of their torn, shabby clothing, that they were such undesirable associates. Wise heads knew that such idle loungers were on the road to wickedness, if they had not already been guilty of crime. Passers-by might now and then hear an oath from their young lips, and the Sunday morning bells did not send them to the pleasant Sabbath-school, or bid them join happy families on their way to church. Two of God's commandments at least they were breaking; they could not be companions which any good mother would wish for her son.

Among the most unfailing frequenters of " the corner" were two brothers, who were known among their friends as "Buster" and "Baby Jim;" what their real names were no one knew, and on this point they were as ignorant as every body else. Ever since they could remember they had been wanderers in the streets of the great city, living by begging, pilfering, or by the doubtful charities of people far gone in wickedness. Just now they had some new acquaintances who seemed to take a great fancy to them. Buster and Baby Jim had found a house where they could always get a comfortable meal, and where rough men gave them a hearty welcome and seemed to take a special pleasure in counting the boys "one of them." Sundry hints had been thrown out as to teaching the brothers how to make a handsome living, and "Baby Jim" was led to believe there was a very easy way for him to lay up stores of money, and ride in his own carriage one

of these days. The little chap could not
help thinking that this would be much
more agreeable than his present diver-
sion of "hanging on behind" in imminent
danger of the coachman's whip, though it
might not be quite as exciting.

Through the day the boys were at the
street corner, lounging and chatting, but
in the evening they were going through
a course of lessons preparatory to the
very profitable branch of business on
which they were expected to enter.

Poor young things; without father or
mother, ignorant and penniless, what
was to prevent them from starting upon
a career of crime, to end in prison or on
the scaffold? They had no true friend
to warn them; no faithful, loving friend
to call them to the ways of pleasantness
and peace, and teach them the joy of
honest labor and the manly satisfaction
of earning their own bread.

As it was, the weeks went by, and
Baby Jim's small face grew more keen,
eager, and cunning in its expression;
while Buster's every limb and feature
spoke of the future ruffian, daily increasing in strength and daring.

There was scarcely a year's difference
between the ages of the boys. They
knew that, though strangers could hardly believe it. They well remembered
when it was their delight to stand side
by side under the projecting shop windows, not an inch's difference in their
height, though Buster even then claimed
authority as the elder brother.

Exposure and hard usage had stunted
little Jim; but his thin wiry figure seemed made of springs of steel, and was
more than a match in strength for many
a taller, sturdier form; yet with Buster
he never presumed to contend. Truly
Buster was too formidable an adversary

for any of the boys lightly to engage him in battle. The big, burly lad was a kind of king among his associates, laying down the law, and sustaining his authority like many another monarch, by the irresistible argument of brute force.

Poor, tempted, sinful street-vagrants as were Buster and Baby Jim, there yet lingered in their hearts one feeling which made them akin, though afar off, to saints and angels, and even proved them lost and wandering children of the God of love.

A true, deep affection for each other had somehow sprung up and been fostered in the midst of the hardening, miserable life they had led. Sharers of the same pangs of hunger and cold, alike neglected by all the world, they had grown doubly dear to each other through sympathy in suffering and loneliness.

Baby Jim lost his keen, old look when

his eye fell admiringly on his brother, and the innocence of infancy and the softness of a woman would for the moment hover in his face, beautifying and purifying it as it spoke out the real love that was stirring within.

It was when Buster's arm was thrown protectingly round his little companion, and only then, that one could catch a glimpse of the better side of his nature. At such times the defiant, swaggering young bully would for the moment show that union of strength and tenderness, of power and forbearance, which gives to a bold and manly character a peculiar charm.

It was perhaps as much to their true affection for each other that the brothers owed their influence among their associates, as to Buster's strength or the ac· knowledged shrewdness of Baby Jim.

What is true, noble, and good must

ever have its power over the most aban-
doned of men.   While the poor straggling vagrants of the street corner mock-
ingly gave to big Buster and little Jim
the name of " the Twins," each young
heart in secret yielded its tribute of
admiration and approval to the faithful
-love of the brothers.

CHAPTER II:

"BUTTER AND EGGS."

ALL that is learned in the world is not gathered from books. A man or boy who will keep his eyes and ears open, will find out much that was never put in print. Many of the lads at the street corner could at the best but spell out a sign, or slowly-read the headings in great letters on an "extra;" yet there was a kind of knowledge afloat among them which had for them its own use, not always of the most innocent kind.

The passers-by did not need to tell these observing boys who they were, or what was their business. A lawyer, a doctor, a merchant, a clerk, or a mechanic was as well known by them at a glance, as if he had his occupation put

on the band of his hat, like the porters
of city hotels. They could distinguish
the up-town from the down-town people, and the "west-enders" from "east-
enders." Plain clothing could not hide
from them the comfortable, easy look of
one who has always had his wants grati-
fied without exertion; nor could the gay-
est finery shut their eyes to the empty
purses of the foolish women who spent
their all to make a fine show upon the
public street. A countryman might try
to look as much at ease as he pleased,
and deck himself in new attire from the
crown of his head to the sole of his feet;
they knew where he came from, without
the help of hob-nailed shoes or homespun
to tell the story.

"Butter and eggs," said Buster to
Baby Jim one day.

Jim followed the direction of his brother's finger, and saw a stout, cheerful-

looking woman coming slowly towards
the group among which he was standing.

"Yes," said Jim, nodding assent.
"First visit to the city. Full purse;
pocket on the left side drops heavy."
The subject of these remarks was quite
unconscious of any thing in her appearance suggestive either of the dairy or
the farm-yard, but of neither would she
have dreamed of being ashamed. She
did not look like a person to be ashamed
of any thing she said or did, at home
or abroad. Her full face, with its rosy
cheeks and wide-open blue eyes, was
beaming with truth and kindliness. She
felt no mortification about her style of
dress truly, though a foolish city belle
would rather have stayed at home from
church every Sunday for a month, than
have worn that odd gray linen cottage bon-
net, or that mouseline de laine, so perfect
a reflection of the flower-garden in June.

Our stranger was perhaps a little proud of her appearance, complacent at least, but not so far as to despise others less fortunate than herself. Her eye softened as it fell on the group of ragged boys, and her hand instinctively sought the left-hand pocket, where, as Jim had rightly judged, her funds were reposing.

Whatever might have been her kindly intention, she was not allowed to carry it out. There was a stir among the boys as she approached, and Jim exclaimed, "Now for it. Who'll get to the next corner first?"

At this challenge the whole party set off at full speed, rushing past the stranger as if borne on the wings of the wind. Unceremoniously crowded and nudged by the rude little crew, the good woman could hardly keep her place on the sidewalk, and the glance she sent after them expressed any thing but approval of their proceedings. Gathering up her dress, she stepped quickly on, making meanwhile mental comparisons between the manners of the city and the country, in which the region of butter and eggs had the decided preference.

At the appointed corner the runners stopped. A smile went round the group as Jim held up a well-filled purse, which in the confusion he had managed to take from the pocket of the country woman.

Buster struck it from his hand to the pavement, exclaiming, "Police! Run for your lives!"

Jim and his companions disappeared down an alley as if made invisible by a spell, while Buster stopped, picked up the purse, and proceeded to examine the contents, as if he felt himself in perfect security. The strong hand of a policeman was laid upon his shoulder, and

there was an exclamation in his ear: "I
saw it all. No lies, youngster; I know
your tricks."

Buster had acted on the impulse of
the moment, prompted by the desire to
save his brother; and now, when he found
himself a prisoner, his courage for a moment forsook him. He knew that his
boasted strength was as nothing com-
pared with the powerful figure of the
policeman. Swift and stinging were the
thoughts that rushed through his mind
as he was hurried rapidly along by his
captor. Already in imagination the grim
cold walls of a prison were closing around
him; already he was cut off from freedom and sunshine, and gazing sadly at
the small barred window whose glimmer
of light cast the only brightness on his
dark lot.

Buster was but a lad, scarce twelve
years old, and big tears forced them-

selves into his eyes as this gloomy picture presented itself to his mind.

The policeman, eager to overtake the
countrywoman, lost no time in examining the face or studying the feelings of
the culprit. Buster's tears were unno-
ticed, and the hardened, sullen look which
he had summoned to conceal his fears
was all that met the eye of the officer
when at length he paused beside the object of his pursuit.

"Is this your purse, madam?" asked
the policeman.

The woman put her hand in her pocket, and then exclaimed, "That it is. I
must have dropped it. I believe I did
take out my handkerchief a piece back."

The little group was here joined by a
gentleman, whose eager inquiries were
soon answered by a full account of the
affair from the policeman, in which he
left no doubt of Buster's guilt. The

stranger was not yet forty years old,
but he had all the dignity and wisdom of
age, united with the fresh, loving sympa-
thies of youth. A thorough Christian in
heart and life, like his divine Master, he
gave to the sinful and unfortunate his
most tender interest.

His glance was full of yearning pity
as it fell on Buster's young face. The
boy looked up suddenly as the stranger
took his hand and said, "I am sorry for
all this, my little fellow. Perhaps it may
not prove so bad as it seems. Suppose
you tell me the truth about it."

"I did n't steal the purse," said Buster, for the first time breaking silence.

"Just as likely as not I dropped it.
I'm not used to having money about me
much," said the woman, now becoming
uneasy and anxious to be through with
the disagreeable scene. "Let the boy
go. I'm to be off in the cars in less

than an hour, and can't stand here talking. Look here, my lad, you are young
to be walking in bad ways. May the
Lord take care of you and keep you out
of sin."

There was real earnestness in the
woman's manner, and as she walked
quickly away, Buster felt as if he were
losing a friend.

"You don't get off so," said the officer. "I know you, and you've got to
stand your trial this time. It may keep
your neck from the gallows to hide in
the jug a while now; so come along with
me, and put on a pleasanter face, if you
can."

The rough, coarse manner of the policeman won from Buster no reply but a
look of blustering defiance, while from
the stranger's glance he turned away, as
if unable to answer its tender pity.

CHAPTER III.

A RIDE.

WE will not follow Buster through the scenes of his trial. He could not be proved guilty of stealing the purse; but he was unable to show that he had any home or lawful way of life, and it was made plain that the men with whom he was known to associate were of the most suspicious kind. He was at the best in training for a course of guilt, and the strong arm of the law was put forth to save the community from one villain more endangering its peace and safety.

Buster was not to be sent to the gloomy prison whose outer walls he had so often surveyed. The stranger, who had followed him, had gained permission to take charge of the young culprit.

Buster soon found himself in a railroad car. He was a prisoner, that was plain, for the stranger kept a kind but firm hold of his wrist until the train started, and resumed it at every stopping-place. There was no present chance of escape, and Buster, with the natural elasticity of youth, began to make the best of the circumstances in which he found himself.

Along the banks of a wide river the swift cars were rapidly flying. The city with its din and bustle was soon left far behind them, and greenness and beauty took the place of brick walls and paved streets. For the first time in his life Buster was in the open country. There was something imposing to him in the wide stretch of the landscape, the blue mountains lining the distant horizon, the noble river tracing its shining way mid hills and meadows, and over all the blue,

majestic arch of the clear summer sky.
A singular sense of littleness and loneliness stole over the heart of the boy. He
felt within him nothing akin to this purity and beauty; and more welcome to
him then would have been a footing in
some narrow filthy lane of the city, than
the sight of nature in its imposing grandeur.

In the excitement that had attended
Buster's capture and trial, he had thought
but little of his brother; but now, as a
lonely yearning crept over him, his little
companion came naturally to his mind.
"Where was Baby Jim? Would he ever
know what had become of Buster?"

The boy's face softened as he dwelt on
this theme, and when the stranger turned
to look at him, he was surprised at the
expression that had taken the place of
his hitherto prevailing look of sullen de-
termination.

"What are you thinking of, my lad? You said you had no home, and did not know who your parents were, or I should fancy you were thinking of your mother."

The gentleman's voice and manner were very kind, and Buster instinctively answered, "I did n't say I had n't any brother."

"So you have a brother. You need not be afraid to talk to me now. Nothing you say will go against you or him. I think you love your brother, from the way you looked when you were thinking of him just now," said the stranger.

"We 've been together always, him and me. He 's a little un, but knowin. I 'm a'most twice as big, but we are near about the same age," said Buster. "It 's kind o' queer to me not to have him along. It 's a lonely place out here, mister; no houses nor nothin."

The conversation thus begun was kept up, until Buster grew so much at his ease that his companion easily won from him the story of Baby Jim's theft, and Buster's impulsive thrusting himself into danger in his stead.

This confession prompted the stranger to two silent prayers. He knew not whither the young thief had fled, but he could follow him with a petition, and beg the God of love to check him in his career of crime, and call him to the paths of virtue and peace. To Buster his heart warmed, and earnestly he prayed that the kind natural feelings lingering in the boy's rough nature might be cherished, and that, sanctified by the Spirit of God, he might yet reflect the likeness of Him who bore our punishment, and was the sufficient sacrifice and satisfaction for the sin of the world.

A sudden checking of the train an-

nounced its approach to another stopping-place.

"We get out here," said Buster's companion; and he led the boy from the car.

A small wagon was in waiting. Apparently they were expected. Side by
side they took their places, and then the
driver started off the horse at an easy
trot.

"Where be you goin to take me?" said
Buster, his curiosity at length finding
vent in words.

"There," said the stranger. "We are
going there."

On the top of a high hill stood a large
stone building, firm and substantial, rising, story upon story, until the upper
windows looked out far, far over the
broad landscape on every side.

"This is to be, for a time at least,
your home," continued Buster's guide.

The boy was silent. Those stone walls

might hide many a dark cell; perhaps there was one in store for him. Yet the word "home" had a cheerful sound; a home the poor lad never had known; he would not banish the pleasant vision that its bare mention had conjured up; he would patiently wait until his fate should be made known to him.

CHAPTER IV.

THE STONE BUILDING.

BUSTER's heart beat fast as he mounted the stone steps that led to the great building that had been pointed out to him.

The door was unlocked, and he entered with his companion.

Through a wide clean hall he passed into a neat, comfortable parlor, with its rocking-chairs, piano, and every mark of comfort.

"You may sit here a few moments," said his companion. "I will return for you shortly."

Buster sat down alone in the large room, then rose, walked round it, astonished to find himself on a carpeted floor and surrounded by so many signs of plenty.

He had hardly completed his survey when his conductor returned. Sitting down by him, the stranger said, "Buster, my boy, you have had enough of a poor, miserable, wicked life. I do n't want you to grow up to sin and shame. I have brought you here to be taught to do right, and to learn to lead an honest, useful, Christian life. There are more than three hundred boys in this building. Some of them, like you, have never had any home, and some have been brought up in wicked homes, where they have never learned any thing good. When they come here, we wash them and put on them clean clothes, and tell them we want them to leave all their dirt and wickedness behind them. My boy, you have heard of the great God who made you. He formed your body by his wonderful power, and he can make your bad heart pure. He can help you to leave off swearing, lying, stealing, Sabbath-breaking, anger, and every wicked way. I want you to kneel down as I do, and I will ask him to help you and make you better, for the sake of his dear Son."

Buster mechanically knelt down, but kept his eyes open and fixed upon his companion's face.

Very earnest was the short, simple prayer that he heard offered for him, and love and sincerity were marked on the countenance of the speaker. "You a'n't a sham, anyhow," said Buster, as the gentleman rose from his knees.

After a moment of silence, he said, "Go now, my boy, with the man you will find standing at the door. He will see that you are properly washed and dressed, and after that I will show you your new home."

"A'n't I going to be shut up? You would n't come it over me?" said Buster.

"You will not be shut up here, if you do as you are told, and behave yourself properly. I have not brought you here to punish you, but to try to make you better," was the reply.

"That's a queer dodge," said Buster; "a first-rate one though," and with a cheerful step he left the room.

More than an hour passed before Buster returned, so completely transformed that Baby Jim would hardly have recognized him. His thick hair had been cropped close to his head, and his browned, begrimed face had been washed until it fairly shone in its cleanliness. Buster moved but awkwardly in his new suit of plain stout clothing, but he looked approvingly at himself as he approached the gentleman whom he now considered quite as an old friend.

"Now a'n't I a beater!" he exclaimed, as he surveyed himself from top to toe.

"You do look greatly improved; I should hardly know you myself. See to it that you leave your badness behind you with those old clothes. Now give me your hand, and I'll show you your way over the building."

"Here is the dining-room," said the gentleman, opening the door to a large hall where several long lines of tables were ranged in regular order. Great slices of bread were piled in pans that were placed along through the centre of the tables, and by each boy's plate stood a bowl of good sweet milk. "Here is where you will eat your supper presently. Do you think you can relish it, Buster?"

"Now that beats every thing. Do them boys all eat here? My!" exclaimed Buster, lost in astonishment and admiration. " Wont I lay in though, when I get a chance."

We will not follow Buster and his guide as they passed through chapel and school-room, bathing-room and work-room, until they reached the large sleeping apartment, when the gentleman again paused to unlock the door. The stranger used his bunch of keys to open every door; this alone gave to Buster the idea of confinement. This was just what was needed to make him feel that though kindly cared for, he was still to be under wise control.

The door of the large dormitory was thrown wide open. Cool breezes came in through the windows, and from white scoured floor to white ceiling the air was pure and sweet as if it was fresh from the mountain-side. Everywhere small white beds were standing in long rows across the room. "These are the beds

for the boys. Here is to be your place,
number 373. That's to be your number. I shall hope to hear every thing
good of 373," said Buster's companion.

Buster looked curiously at the bed, and
slowly turned down the spread, examining every article of the covering; then
he exclaimed, "You do n't mean I am to
sleep in there! why, I sha'n't never want
to get up. My! but it's soft." Buster
sat down suddenly on the edge of the
bed, and looking up into the face of his
friend, he said, "What makes you do
so? What makes you get us boys and
serve us so, instead of lickin us all to
pieces, or shuttin us up in the jug, or
just kickin us and lettin us go?"

"Buster," began the stranger, "listen
to me and I will answer your question
truly." The boy's attention was caught,
and his heart softened. He listened—
listened with tears in his eyes, as he

heard the story of the Saviour's love, how He came to seek and to save that which was lost, and had bidden his true followers to go and do likewise.

"And you do it. You go into it strong," said Buster as his companion ceased speaking. Rough and unsuitable as seemed his comment, he yet had felt and understood what had been said to him.

"You will try, my boy, to learn to be better, wont you?" said the gentleman.

"I wish Baby Jim was in that 'ere bed, long side o' mine. Then I could turn in, and feel about right," said Buster, following out his own train of thought.

"When you go to bed every night, kneel down by that bed, and say, 'God bless me, and help me to be a good boy, for Christ's sake. God bless my brother Jim, and help him to be a good boy;' and may-be it will all come out right before you expect it. The great God who sees you and me, sees your little brother, and can watch over him and keep him from evil."

"I was n't thinkin about keepin him from evil; he takes to that most too nat-'ral. I wish I had him though, there in that bed, and I 'd tell him I 'd thrash the skin off from him if he did n't mind just what you say; for I hold to it, you are the right kind of a man, just uncommon different from any I ever come across before. Eh, do you think it 's about time for them boys to be layin in with the bread and milk? I 'm ready."

Buster folded his hands that evening with more than three hundred boys, while the blessing of God was asked on the simple bountiful meal before them. Very heartily prayed his friend that poor Buster might be fed with the bread from heaven, and lay hold on eternal life.

CHAPTER V.

THE HON. MR. B——.

IT was hard for Buster to accommo-
date himself to the regular life of his
new abode. To eat and sleep, go out
and come in, study and play, lie down
and rise up, work and stop working, by
the clock, were new things indeed, after
the wandering habits into which the poor
boy had fallen. Yet to all this he became by degrees accustomed, and even
this outward training took from him
somewhat of the wild, reckless air which
had marked him before. In the work-
room and in the class, Buster showed
any thing but stupidity, and yet the
friend who had placed him in this kindly
asylum was still anxiously watching for
some more satisfactory signs of improve-

ment. In vain he inquired, week after
week, for good news about Buster. The
boy often proved turbulent and unman-
ageable, and more than once he had un-
dergone the severest punishments in use
at the institution. Buster was, through
the force of circumstances, slightly al-
tered; but it was plain that he needed
but to be exposed again to temptation,
to fall back into all his evil practices.

Buster had been for several months at
the asylum, when the boys were one day
summoned to the chapel at an unusual
hour. In they marched to the sound of
music, keeping time, and stepping as
truly as well-trained soldiers. Leading
one of the long files came Buster, his
head erect and his great black eyes wandering hither and thither as if asking
what was the provocation for this extra-
ordinary assembly.

The boys were hardly seated when the

superintendent introduced to them the Hon. Mr. B—— of Ohio. At a given signal they all rose and politely acknowledged the introduction.

Mr. B—— was a splendid specimen of Christian manhood. His tall and strongly built figure at once attracted Buster's attention and won his unqualified approval; nor could the boy help owning to himself that the face of the stranger was as attractive as his well-knit form.

The many voices of the children blended in a cheerful hymn of praise, and as Mr. B—— listened to the holy words they so sweetly sang, the unbidden tears clouded his eyes. Rank upon rank, line upon line, rose the heads of the singers. In thought Mr. B—— wandered to the scenes of vice and misery from which these poor children had been rescued, and angels' work indeed it seemed to him to have gathered these neglected outcasts and taught them even with the lips to praise the God of heaven. In a kind of touching recitative rose those beautiful words of commendation which the Lord is said to address to those on his right hand at the day of judgment. When the children came to the closing sentence, "Inasmuch as ye have done it unto one of the least of these my brethren, ye have done it unto me," Mr. B—— could almost imagine the Saviour bodily present among them and speaking himself the sacred words that came from the lips of the singers.

A Saviour near at hand he seemed; and when Mr. B—— rose to call upon him in prayer, he spoke to him as One in the midst of them, yearning with his almighty heart of love fully to take to his bosom these the least of his flock, yet precious above all price in his eyes.

When the prayer was over, Mr. B——

knew that he was expected to make an address to the children. In many public places and before many critical audiences had his eloquent voice been heard, yet now there was a sense of choking in his throat, and a growing feeling of inability to say what he wished to the young hearers before him. Like the Syrophenician woman, he humbly prayed in silence, "Lord, help me." He felt that the message must come from God, if it should be blessed to do the work for which he was yearning.

The superintendent glanced at Mr. B——, and saw by the working of his fine face that just now he was too much moved to give vent to his feelings in words.

"Boys," began the superintendent, "let me tell you that the gentleman who is to speak to you to-day has spoken to thousands of men, of grown men, and

they have listened with delighted attention. In the State he comes from, he is
looked up to more than if he were the
governor. I like to show him to you as
a Christian gentleman, one to whom God
has given health, talent, and wealth, and
he delights to use them all to work for
his heavenly Master. Boys, listen to Mr.
B——. It may never fall to your lot to
hear such a man again."

Mr. B—— stepped out beyond the
desk which stood upon the raised plat-
form where he had been sitting. With
his powerful figure in full sight, and his
strongly-marked kindly face looking lovingly upon them, he began.

"My lads, your superintendent has
spoken in my praise. Let us grant that
what he has said is true, true as far as
the world knows any thing of me; yet in
my closet I must bow the knee and cry
like you, 'God be merciful to me a sin-

ner.' Boys, I will tell you a story. I
knew a child once, a poor, wandering,
homeless child, who had no mother to
rock him on her knee, no father to earn
him daily bread. His little tender hands
soon learned to steal, his baby lips could
speak an oath and laugh while he was
speaking. What wonder that he grew in
wickedness as he gained in years? I will
not tell you how he went from step to
step, till his young heart was hardened
in sin. Perhaps some of you may know
too well the evil path he trod. That path
ended, as it must surely end, in *misery*.
He found himself shut up within damp,
gloomy prison walls. No pleasant sunshine to cheer him now; no friendly
voice to bid him take courage. Two
long years he was to spend in dreary
confinement. He bowed his head upon
his hands and cried as if his heart would
break. There were no rough compan-

ions round him now to laugh at his bitter
tears. There was no gentle hand to wipe
those tears away. Alone, alone in his
guilty misery sat the wicked orphan-boy.
So the wretched days and weeks came
and went. One morning there was a vis-
itor in his lonely cell. A kind motherly
face was bending over the poor hardened
boy. He would not answer her gentle
words; he would not look into her loving eyes. Yet she came again and again.
Sickness seized upon the weak frame of
the prisoner. She nursed him as tenderly as if he had been one of the sweet children of her own comfortable home. She
made him love her; he could not help it;
and when by and by she talked to him
of the precious Saviour who had sent her
to his side, he learned to love that Saviour too.

"One long year passed, and then another, and at last the prisoner was free

once more. He might go where he would, and find for himself a home. Did he turn back to the wretched alleys he knew? Did he seek the old sinners who had led him astray before? No; he had his Bible in his hand and his God overhead. There was no such path for him now. Straight for the open country he went. On, on he walked, till the city was far behind him. He used his right hand for honest labor by day, by night he continued his journey. In the wide West he found a resting-place. No one knew him there. There he began his new life. God had forgiven him for Christ's sake, and he could cheerfully bear poverty and hard work, knowing that he had a sure home in heaven.

"God blessed that poor lad, and gave him friends and a home and wealth, and even some share of this world's honors. He stands before you now, and thanks

his heavenly Father for all his mercies.
I have been telling you my own life, my
boys. I know what it is to be poor and
homeless and tempted and wicked. These
are strong enemies, but God is stronger.
He can help you, if you will but fight on
the right side. God can cleanse you and
strengthen you and bring you off conquerors. He will forgive you for the
sake of his dear Son who died on the
cross for you. He will help you to lead
a new life. You will have a hard struggle for it, but you will win if you fight
bravely. The coward gains no battle.
He who is afraid to begin, will never end
with honor. My dear boys, let this day
be, at least for one of you, the most im-
portant day you have ever known. Go
in secret to the great God of heaven.
Ask him, for his Son's sake, to blot out
all your sins, and help you to live a new
and better life.

"May the Holy Spirit bless to you these words of mine; and when you shall have triumphed over sin and shame, may you take poor wandering children by the hand, and lead them to the feet of Jesus. Let us pray." ·

As sincerely, humbly, earnestly, and trustfully as when he first knelt at the feet of Jesus, Mr. B—— now sought forgiveness for himself and the children in whose name he spoke. One young heart, at least, went with him. For the first time, Buster prayed, "God be merciful to me a sinner. Cleanse thou me, and I shall be clean. Wash me, and I shall be whiter than snow."

To Buster it now seemed possible that even for such as he there was an upward path. God helping him, from this day forward he would leave his evil deeds behind him, and strive to be a true servant of Christ.

CHAPTER VI.

PARTING.

WE have seen the beginning of a Christian life, the tiny grain of mustard-seed taking root in poor Buster's heart. This was the commencement of a good work, but it was truly only the commencement. Mr. B—— had rightly said the struggle was a hard one. Old habits and old temptations would rise again when they seemed almost conquered, and new faults sprung up where others had been subdued. Yet Buster persevered.

Two years Buster continued at the Asylum, before his kind friends dared to trust him away from their watchful eyes and timely counsel. At length there was a new party of boys starting for the West, to find homes among the farmers of the fast growing states. Buster's name was on the list. As Buster he still was known, but in solemn baptism he had taken the Christian name of Paul. He chose to be called after the great apostle, who, though counting himself the chief of sinners, had yet through the grace of God become among the chief of saints.

Again Buster was to take a journey, far, far longer than the ride in the swift cars that had brought him to his late home. What a change had been wrought in him since, rough, wicked, and reckless, he entered those sheltering walls. The friend who had then been his guide was now with him to bid him farewell.

Buster took the hand that was stretched out to him, and grasping it in both of his, he exclaimed, "God will bless you, sir. I can't thank you. I don't know how to say what I feel. I owe every thing to you. I'll try to do you credit.

May-be you'll hear of me one of these days."

"I trust I shall see you at the right hand of God, rejoicing among the redeemed," said his companion with great earnestness. "Be watchful and humble, my lad. Hold fast to your Bible. Be faithful in prayer. Resist the very beginnings of evil, the angry look, the profane word, the touching of the slightest trifle that is not your own. God bless you, and bring you off conqueror."

"Thank you," said Buster, humbly. "But Oh, sir, you will keep a watch for *him?* May-be he'll turn up yet. Remember, blue eyes, and curly brown hair, small and slender, and an old, smart look in his face. That's he, that's Baby Jim."

What was it that unnerved the great strong boy? His hands trembled as they gave that final grasp at parting. Ah, the

Christian brother but yearned the more tenderly for the companion of his childhood, and longed to know him snatched from those evil paths whose end is death.

"I will pray for him, and watch for him, my boy. Trust him to the Lord, and labor to be a brother who shall be a fit guide and example for him when we shall have found him."

Buster heard the parting words, and answered, "Aye, aye, that's what I will." Then with another "good-by," he sprang into the cars that were to bear him away to the scene of his future life.

CHAPTER VII.

A WESTERN FARMER.

AMONG the thirty lads who were starting for the West, there was not one more
full of hope than was the tall stout boy
whom we have known as Buster. As
mile after mile was left behind him, he
breathed more and more freely. Sepa-
rated from the scenes of his early guilt,
he felt it to be more and more possible
for him to lead the life he desired.

Where would his lot fall? What home
would be his? To these questions Buster could give no answer; but he found
vent for the feelings of his heart by singing in a low voice the hymn,

> "Father, whate'er of earthly bliss
> Thy sovereign will denies,
> Accepted at thy throne of grace,
> Let this petition rise

"Give me a calm, a thankful heart,
From every murmur free;
The blessings of thy grace impart,
And let me live to thee.

"Let the sweet hope that I am thine
My life and death attend;
Thy presence through my journey shine,
And crown my journey's end."

Buster's hymn attracted no attention amid the Babel of sounds made by the excited, rejoicing boys. The kind friend who had charge of them did not check the natural outburst of their feelings, but sat among them enjoying the various ways in which they chose to manifest their glee.

Somewhat sobered down by the long journey, the boys at length reached their first stopping-place, at a small town in the centre of a rich farming country. They were expected, that was plain; for many rough wagons were tied along the principal street, while their owners joined the deputation of the citizens who were at the dépôt to give the young strangers a welcome.

On the large public square an agricultural fair had lately been held, and the seats provided for the ladies were still standing. On these the boys were placed, while an abundant luncheon was passed round for their refreshment. Then followed some singing by the children, and a speech from the gentleman who had them in charge. He simply stated the plan of the institution from which they had come, and offered to the farmers assembled an opportunity of sharing in the Christlike work of redeeming these poor wanderers from a life of want and crime, and training them in honest homes. Wherever they went, they were to be received as members of the family. They were to be encouraged to show by their conduct what they were, forgetting

whence they came and what they had
been.

While the gentleman was speaking,
many scrutinizing eyes were fixed upon
the eager faces of the boys. Up and
down before the rising seats walked a
small short man, with his head on one
side as he looked systematically at every
boy, allowing to each his fair time to
make an agreeable impression. It was
evident that the good man was seeking
a new member for his household, and
meant to be careful in the selection.
The process seemed to be an exciting
one, for he soon took off his homespun
coat and threw it over his arm, and
pushed his felt hat back on his head, so
that his wide forehead might have the
full benefit of the breeze. There was
shrewdness in his small clear blue eyes
and long, sharp nose ; but the quizzical,
kindly expression about the mouth was

sufficient to reassure the stranger who might at first be afraid to find him close at a bargain. He soon became a great favorite among the boys, and cries of "Take me," "I'm the chap for you," sounded out from the lines as he pursued his methodical examination.

Before Buster the little farmer at length made a decided stand. "Would I suit you? Do you think you could close hands with me?" he said confidentially.

Buster reached his big hand over the heads of the little boys below him, and gave the inquirer a hearty grasp as he replied, "First-rate."

"All settled," said the farmer, going back to the crowd and listening as faithfully to the concluding remarks of the speaker as if he intended to report them for the county newspaper. A report of the speech he knew he would have to

give to one person at least, and that a
party whom he was far more anxious to
please than the uncertain public, who
might applaud to-day and decry to-morrow.

"My Mrs. Jillard," as he was wont to
call his wife, would demand a circum-
stantial account of that day's proceedings, he was sure, and he meant to be
prepared upon at least one department
in which he would be examined.

No objection being made to Mr. Jillard's selection by the gentleman in charge
of the boys, the worthy farmer seemed
inclined to carry off his prize at once.

"Then we may as well be moving,"
he exclaimed, taking Buster protectively
by the arm. Buster was a full half head
taller than his new acquaintance, and
would have been a dangerous enemy for
him in a pitched battle; and the big boy
could hardly help smiling at the tender,

careful way in which he was taken in
hand.   .

Mr. Jillard had proposed the move,
and yet he lingered and kept fumbling
meditatively in his coat pocket. It was
plain that he felt he was making a bargain in which the advantage was too
much on his side, and yet he did not
know how to mend the matter. At length
he broke out, "It seems as if I ought to
do something. I don't like to pay money. That looks ugly, as if I bought the
boy. But see here; may n't I give you
something to go to clothing and feeding
some poor little chap that's just picked
out of the gutter, and is n't fit to be let
loose on honest folks? Hicks Jillard
would like to have that ten dollar note
put to that account.' Will that be all
right?"

Mr. Jillard's contribution was cheerfully received, and he had the promise

of a letter describing the boy for whose benefit it should be used.

"Now for it," said the farmer; and starting off at a round rate, he soon made Buster realize that he would have to be a fast walker if he kept up with him.

At a post where two quiet farm-horses were tied, Mr. Jillard stopped. "Were you ever on a horse, boy? What's your name?"

"Never, but I should n't mind trying," said Buster, his eyes sparkling.

"What's your name?" repeated the questioner.

"Buster I've always been called; but I was baptized Paul just before I left home," said the boy.

"Baptized; I like that," said Mr. Jillard. "A good beginning. Hold to it, and do n't go backwards. Breaking is dangerous in boys as well as horses.

Paul Jillard, that's your name. Can you write?"

"Yes, sir," said Buster promptly.

"Then write Paul Jillard in your books. Don't cut P. J. now everywhere, as if you owned all the world and wanted to put your mark on it. I don't hold to that. Knives have their uses; but this cutting of letters round is putting good tools to a bad job. Yes, Paul Jillard is your name, but I shall call you Buster, because you are used to it; my Mrs. Jillard may do as she pleases. Now get up on to that horse as quick as you can. She'll be expecting us."

Buster made several vain attempts to mount from the ground, while Mr. Jillard looked on laughing till his eyes were full of tears. "There, now, why can't you do as I do?" said the farmer, hopping lightly to the back of the other tall horse.

Buster watched the operation closely,

and managed to follow at once with a tolerable imitation.

"Here, so," said Mr. Jillard, telling Buster how to hold the reins. "Sit steady. Do n't be afraid."

With no further preface or preparation, Mr. Jillard started off his horse at a round trot, and its "match" briskly kept it company. Buster had his own qualms as he felt himself fairly borne along without the exercise of his own will; but he was determined to acquit himself bravely, and did not once call out for quarter during the five minutes in which the unmerciful trotting was kept up.

"Now we 'll take it slower," said Mr. Jillard, slackening his own pace. "You 'll feel easier for finding you can ride fast without falling off. We 've ten miles before us, so we must n't tire out too much at the start."

By the time the ten miles were over, Buster felt as if he and Mr. Jillard were old acquaintances. All dread of meeting the farmer's wife had been overcome by various remarks concerning her which the proud husband had let fall during the ride. In his heart Buster already thanked God that the lines had fallen unto him "in pleasant places."

CHAPTER VIII.

MRS. JILLARD.

MR. JILLARD'S farm had no fanciful
name. It had never been called Wood-
land, after the primeval forest that tow-
ered just beyond the wheat-fields, nor
Clear-springs, for the bright water that
welled up on every hill-side and danced
its way to the valleys below. Mr. Jillard
was content to talk about "our house,"
without having the great red wooden
building photographed to put at the head
of his letters or to frame and hang in his
clean parlor.

It was just sunset when Buster's first
ride on horseback was over, and his
"gallant steed" walked quietly into a
barn-yard and held up his head at his
accustomed post. Buster would have

found dismounting a stiff and awkward
business, if Mr. Jillard had not come to
him, saying, "I'll help you to-day; next
time you must get down as spry as I
do."

Just as Buster stood fairly on the
ground, his attention was fixed by a figure which came round the corner of the
barn. Mrs. Jillard had been milking,
and in each hand she held a full bucket,
which showed her abundant success.
Thus doubly balanced, she could move
but slowly, a gait which well suited her
tall, comely figure. Her round face was
pink with the flush of health, and the
kindly dimples were dotting her cheeks
as she exclaimed,

"Home again, Hicks. You are a
punctual fellow. And this is the boy.
You are right welcome, my lad. Here,
take the buckets, Hicks, and let me shake
him by the hand."

Buster stood aghast as that kind honest face beamed full upon him. He too well remembered it. The scene at the street corner rushed back upon his memory. The cry, "Butter and eggs," the race, the arrest, all, all were present to him.

"Bashful, I suppose. Poor boy," said Mrs. Jillard to her husband, as Buster hung down his head and did not offer to take the outstretched hand.

"There's no accounting for boys," said the farmer in a low voice. "Why, we've been just like chums all along the way. I never saw anybody either that didn't take to you before. I believe he's tired all to pieces, and just feels it getting off the horse. Supper'll make him all right."

Neither supper nor Mrs. Jillard's kind efforts to draw him into conversation could bring all right with poor Buster

He was glad when he was sent off to his sleeping quarters, to get rid of his supposed fatigue and consequent shyness.

"This is to be your room, Buster," said Mrs. Jillard, as she opened the door into a small chamber, the very picture of neatness and comfort. "Stay in it as much as you please, when you are not at work; but leave your boots at the door; that will keep the floor clean, you see. Good-night, my boy. Don't forget your prayers. May God bless you in your new home."

Poor Buster! every added word of kindness was as a dagger sending another pang to his bleeding heart.

Mrs. Jillard set the candle down on the small bureau, and withdrew. Buster turned the button which was the only fastening to the door, and then he bowed his head upon his hands, in utter misery. Here, where he had hoped to begin a

new, an honest, and an honored life, his
sins had found him out. In the home
where he had been so warmly received,
he must ever be reminded of his guilty
career. It could be no pure and perfect
home to him. In the bitterness of his
spirit, he longed for those heavenly mansions where sin and sorrow are known
no more, and where nothing can be laid
to the charge of God's elect, who are for
ever clothed in the white robes of the
righteousness of Christ. Faint-hearted,
he sank down in despair. He could not,
through long years, bear the burden of
his sin and shame, and the deep cry of
his soul was, "Oh that I had wings, like
a dove! for then would I fly away, and
be at rest."

Slowly, very slowly, comfort came to
Buster. In grateful humility, he was at
length enabled to see that it was little,
comparatively, that he should here be

even branded as having once belonged
to a gang of young villains, while his
eternal punishment had been laid upon
One who had for his sake been willing·
to be nailed to the cruel cross. Relying
on that Saviour, he would go forward on
his pilgrimage, striving to bear patiently
his appointed trials.

But would Mrs. Jillard tolerate him
under her roof? It was plain she had
not yet recognized him. Was he so al-
tered that she might never remember to
have seen him before? Would it be just
and right to be daily receiving her kindness with such a secret in his heart? It
had been specially agreed that no questions should be asked of the boys as to
their past lives: why should Mrs. Jillard
be an exception?

It was in vain that Buster so reasoned
with himself. There was a something
within him which prompted him to tell

the whole truth, and abide the consequences. The party which he had accompanied to the West were to remain for some days at the neighboring town, and there would still be an opportunity, for Mr. Jillard to make another selection, and for Buster to obtain another situation. Such a *home* it was not likely would be again open to him. Perhaps Mrs. Jillard would not cast him out. He could but try the effect of a plain statement of the truth, and this he determined to do, as soon as the morrow should dawn.

What a privilege it seemed to Buster, that night, to speak to his merciful Saviour, who knew both his sins and his repentance; who, pure himself, could yet love his wandering children with an everlasting love.

Poor Buster saw, ere he slept, that much of human ambition had mingled with his desire to lead a new, unsullied life. He had hoped to make a great and honorable name in the West; now he should be thankful if as a forgiven penitent, he might have the loving shelter of a retired, kindly, Christian home.

CHAPTER IX.

THE CONFESSION.

BUSTER's sorrowful, anxious thoughts did not prevent him from having sound, refreshing sleep. The glimmer of early dawn recalled him to himself, and to the anticipation of the painful duty before him. Earnestly the poor boy prayed that morning that he might be sustained by the consciousness of the continual presence of the loving Saviour, and so bear whatever measure of deserved humiliation and sorrow might be in store for him.

"What, up already?" said Mr. Jillard, as he heard a stirring in Buster's room as he passed. "That's a good sign. When you are dressed, come down stairs, my lad, and we'll have prayers at once.

Mrs. Jillard has got our breakfast ready, I'll warrant. She's the early bird."

In the large clean kitchen Mr. and Mrs. Jillard were sitting when Buster made his appearance. They were side by side, and together looking over the pages of a great Bible, as if to decide where to begin in their morning reading. "Have you ever read the Bible through, my boy?" said the farmer, as if to call the new inmate into the family counsel.

"No, sir, not all through; but I know the place where it tells a fellow to speak the truth, and that's what I want to do, right straight, no matter what becomes of me." Buster was evidently excited. His shy and awkward manner of the evening before had gone, and a strange haunting memory of something in the past flitted across Mrs. Jillard's mind, as she looked full into his troubled face.

"Speak out, and never fear," said the

kind host. "This is your home, and the very place to tell what's troubling you."

Mr. Jillard spoke warmly, but there was a sad misgiving at his heart that he was going to hear something that would give him a disagreeable surprise.

We will not follow Buster through his short, painful story. He did not hide the fact that though he did not steal the purse, he had been familiar with deeds of the kind, and merely chanced that time not to be the real culprit. The remembrance of the boy he had been was full upon him, and he could not too strongly express his sense of his worthless, guilty condition. "It can't hurt Baby Jim now, ma'am, for me to tell the whole truth out here. He's likely done worse than that by this time, and has, may-be, had no friend to show him better. I've told you all, just what I was when you saw me and I saw you. It is

right you should know. I think you 'd
find me another fellow now, but you
must make your choice. I can go back
and join the boys there, and may-be
somebody else would choose me; but I
know no other place could be like this."

Buster stopped. "Poor boy!" exclaimed honest Mrs. Jillard. "My heart
ached for you when I turned my back
on you, for I saw they were not going to
let you off. It feels tenderer still to you
now. Go away from here! Indeed you
sha'n't. You shall stay, and be an honest western farmer. It was just thinking of those little fellows I saw when I
was in the city that made me tell Hicks,
When that lot of boys comes through here
you must take one, and we 'll do by him
as if he were our own, and God will add
his blessing. That was what I said,
was n't it, Hicks? We 'll stand by it,
wont we?"

Hicks Jillard had been perfectly silent while all this was going on, but now it was his turn to speak, and he stood up to give his words their full force. "I had a good mother, a real pious, smart woman. She set me right when I first put my two feet on the floor, and told me what was what and which way to walk. She folded my two hands, and made me pray at her knee before even I knew what the good words meant. I had the best kind of a bringing up; but the Lord have mercy upon me! where would I be if, at the judgment-day, the wickedness of my boyhood was to stand against me? Many a wrong thing I did which it cuts me to think of now, I who had the right way just chalked out for me, and nothing to do but let her that loved me lead me along in it. It little becomes me to be hard on *you*, my poor boy. God bless them that took you in

and made you with His help what you
are. May we be just a father and mother
to you. That's all I have to say. Your
name I told you was Paul Jillard. I believe you'll do credit to it yet; and if
you should n't, I'll never be sorry I gave
you my right hand and called you my
son. Here, let me hear if you can say
'father,' and 'mother' too. A'n't she a
woman any boy might be proud to call
mother?"

Poor Buster almost shrunk away as he
said, "I a'n't fit. You are too good to
me."

"We a'n't any of us fit. We all have
what's too good for us. We ought all to
be on our knees thanking God for the
least of his mercies to us, and asking him
to help us do our duty to one another.
Let us pray."

That was a real prayer, a true, faithful speaking to God on the part of every

member of the kneeling group. When Buster rose, it was as if a great load had been rolled from his soul.

When he went off to his work that morning, Mrs. Jillard called out cheerily, "Good-by, my son ; look out for your father, and do n't let him drink out of that cool spring when he 's overheated."

"Aye, aye, mother," was Buster's reply.

Mother! What a thrilling, lingering, soothing echo that word called up in the heart of the once wandering orphan-boy.

CHAPTER X.

LETTERS.

BUSTER had been three months at the farm, when Mr. Jillard called him to his side one evening, and said, "I got a letter when I was up in town yesterday. May-be you'd like to have me read it to you. It is from the gentleman who brought you boys out here. So sit down there and listen."

Hicks Jillard had not wasted his time at school, and he was not ashamed to read before any body; indeed, it was rather a pleasure to him, he thought he did the thing so well. In a clear voice he began:

"MR. JILLARD:

"DEAR SIR—You may perhaps remember the ten dollars you gave me to use

for purposes connected with our society."
"I wish it had been twenty," interposed
the reader. "I want to tell you how it
has lately been appropriated. A few
weeks ago, one of our citizens was awak-
ened at night by some one entering his
open window, which was at the back of
the house. He drew a pistol from under
his pillow, and shot at once at the spot
from whence the noise proceeded. There
was a sound of something falling into the
little yard below. The gentleman sprang
up, summoned the police from the front
window, and then hastily dressing himself, went to the yard. There he found
the apparently lifeless figure of a little
boy, who had been employed by older
villains to climb the light grape-trellis
under the window, that he might either
steal for them, or give them an entrance
into the house. The guilty rascals ran
off, leaving the poor little fellow to his

fate; one of them, however, was after-
wards taken, and through him the police
are on the scent of the whole gang. The
boy was badly injured. His right arm
had to be amputated, as inflammation set
in when he was wounded; and in addi-
tion his whole frame was so jarred and
bruised by the fall, that he will be a sad
cripple for life. He does not sit up at
all yet. We have him at the asylum,
and are doing all we can to bring about
a cure of mind and body. Your kind
donation has been applied to his benefit,
and I am sure you will feel a special interest in him and give him the help of
your prayers. We do not know his name.
When asked to tell it, he said he never ·
had any; folks called him just what they
liked, and changed it pretty often too. I
am glad to hear that Buster is doing so
well. We never sent out a boy in whom
we had more confidence. Tell him his

last letter was read to all the boys, and
they were greatly interested in it.   He
must let us know from time to time how
he is getting on.

"Yours very truly."

Mr. Jillard had had a very attentive
listener, and when he closed, Buster burst
forth, "Oh, Mr. Jillard, if that should be
Baby Jim!   That was what they were
getting him ready for; I knew it very
well, though they never said it in words.
Wont you write and ask just how he
looks? I sha'n't rest till I know certainly
about it."

The very day after the arrival of Mr.
Jillard's letter, Buster himself had one
from the friend who understood better
than any one else his deep anxiety for
his brother.   It was as follows.

"DEAR BUSTER—I believe we have
found him.   I have been on the watch
for him ever since we parted.   I think

we have Baby Jim with us, though he will not own to the name. He was badly wounded, as you heard through the letter to Mr. Jillard, and if he ever recovers he will be without his right arm, and crippled otherwise. I wish I could tell you something hopeful about his mind. He seems hardened and indifferent, and all the kindness we have shown does not appear to have moved him at all. Don't be discouraged, my boy; God has so far answered your prayers : persevere, and he may yet give them a perfect fulfilment. You will wonder why I am sure that it is Baby Jim. He corresponds to your description, and when I first called 'Baby Jim' in his presence, he started and was much confused. The poor child seems constantly fearing detection, and afraid to speak out frankly. I told him we once had a boy here named Buster, whom we all loved. You should have seen his eyes open and glisten, when I spoke of you. Yet he was perfectly silent, and has never asked me a question about you. Perhaps it would be well for you to write to him."

Buster did not need to have it twice suggested to him that he should write to his long lost brother. Again and again he wrote, but received no word from Baby Jim.

Buster heard that he listened in silence while his brother's letters were read to him, keeping his face covered with his only hand so that no one could see the working of his poor pale features, but never offered to send even a message in return. This was a hard time for Buster. He longed to go at once to see Baby Jim, and strive to bring up in his eyes that pleasant old look of other days. He knew the thing was impossible, and did not dare to speak out the yearning that was daily increasing, until it was almost uncontrollable.

"Our Buster is worth two common boys," said Mr. Jillard one day, while talking with a neighbor. "I never saw the lad like him for work; so steady too."

This praise, spoken in his hearing, was very welcome to Buster; it had for him a double value. That evening he said to Mr. Jillard, "Do you really think I am a good worker?"

"Indeed I do," was the hearty reply.

"May-be I could do the work of two boys, if I were to try. I'd be willing. I'd get up early and keep on after night. If I could do for him and me, and had a place where I could keep him and see him sometimes. The loft in the barn Baby Jim would think plenty good. Nobody need be troubled with him. If we could only get him here." "Pshaw, Bus-

ter, you'd kill yourself for that boy,"
said Mr. Jillard. "My Mrs. Jillard
wouldn't rest with a poor cripple sleeping in her barn, while she was on the
feather-bed her mother gave her when
she was married. Be industrious, my
boy, and there's no knowing what you
may be able to do when you are a man..
We'll see; we'll see."

"When you are a man!" That seemed a dreary distant time to Buster. Who
could understand the impatient yearning
of his impulsive young spirit?

CHAPTER XI.

THE TEMPTED.

MR. JILLARD had been selling some of
his fine cattle. He had been paid in
gold. Buster had seen the money counted out on the kitchen-table. He knew
where it was locked up for safe keeping.
He knew where the key of the corner
cupboard was hidden in a tea-cup on a
high shelf in the pantry. Sad, sad knowledge for Buster. Why was it that it
haunted him after he lay down to sleep?
Why did the glimmer of the gold contin-
ually glitter before his eyes? He jumped
up and thrust his head out into the cool
air to calm his fevered brain. He but
saw how low was the window, how easy
to jump from it and be far away before
the morning light. With that bag of

gold, what might he not do for Baby
Jim? Once his own master, he would
take charge of his little brother, and
teach him to lead an honest Christian life.

So whispered the tempter, and Buster
listened, listened till in fancy he had the
treasure in his hands and was speeding
over the fields with his ill-gotten gains.
The sins of his youth had risen up to claim
Buster as their victim. Would he fall?

Ah, there was One stronger than the
great adversary on the side of the tempted boy. There was a power mightier
than the force of old habits, or the deceitful allurement of doing evil that good
might come. One who had suffered being tempted, was able to succor him when
he was tempted. He had a High-priest
who is touched with a feeling of our in-
firmities, and he therefore dared to come
boldly to the throne of grace to find help
in his time of need.

Buster turned quickly from the window and threw himself upon his knees. "God be merciful to me a sinner. Christ save me. Help, or I perish," he cried in the anguish of his spirit.

Deep and sincere was his repentance for having allowed his mind to be sullied even for a moment by such guilty thoughts. Now for the first time he realized how great had been his want of faith in feeling that he must take charge of his brother in person, or else all would go wrong. He saw that safer far would be Baby Jim in the keeping of a merciful Saviour, than under the most watchful care of his weak and tempted brother. To that Saviour he now committed him in perfect trust. Having cast his care on Him who is ready to bear all our burdens, Buster lay down to sleep, more calm and hopeful than he had been for many a long day.

CHAPTER XII.

BUSINESS IN TOWN.

BUSTER was roused the next morning at an early hour by an unusual stir in the house. Mrs. Jillard might be heard flying hither and thither, and there was a lumbering sound, as of heavy articles being moved, while the farmer and his wife were deep in earnest conversation.

"Now, Buster, up with you, and be down as quick as you can," said Mr. Jillard's voice at the foot of the stairs. "We must be off for town as soon as we can. I have business to do there, and shall want you with me."

Buster was not to go on horseback this day. Mr. Jillard's long wagon was put in requisition for the trip, and Buster was promised the pleasure of driving a pair for the first time in his life. The bag of gold was brought out, and Buster soon concluded that to deposit this treasure in the bank was the object of the trip. Mrs. Jillard favored her good husband with many parting injunctions, such as, "Be careful. Remember you are not a woman." This last caution Buster could not help thinking was particularly inappropriate, when he remembered how easy it had been to rob a certain honest woman on her first trip to the city.

It was no temptation to Buster now to see the bag of gold counted over once more before his eyes. He did not covet one single dollar of it. He was thankful that the miserable suggestions of the conquered enemy were not again presented to his mind. He had placed his little brother in the care of One who can command the riches of the earth for his wise purposes, and make even kings do his bidding.

Mrs. Jillard at the last moment came staggering under the burden of a monstrous bundle, which she rolled in on the clean straw in the wagon.

Buster wondered much what it could contain, but he asked no questions, sure that Mr. Jillard would only give him a mysterious joking answer. Hicks Jillard did not like to have even his Mrs. Jillard too curious as to his plans and projects.

Straight to the bank drove the farmer, as soon as he entered the town. When the money was deposited, he turned his horses' heads towards the railroad dépôt, and then stood anxiously awaiting the arrival of the train.

"Company coming to our house?" Buster ventured to inquire.

"May-be," was the laconic answer.

There was the welcome whistle at last,

then the black locomotive was seen far down the narrow valley through which the road was built. Hicks Jillard jumped into the wagon, untied the bundle and arranged some pillows and bed-quilts to his satisfaction, and then was down again in a moment, so as to be at his place when the train fairly stopped.

Anxiously he passed his eye along the line of cars; at length he seemed to see the object he desired. At a side-door a strong man appeared carrying a crippled boy. Buster needed no prompting now. He sprang to receive the precious burden in his arms, exclaiming, "Baby Jim! I should have known him anywhere."

The poor little fellow dropped his head upon Buster's shoulder, and cried like a baby.

"You know me, don't you? You know Buster? You ha'n't forgot me?" said the big brother in appealing tones.

"All right," murmured little Jim, clinging the closer to the stout arms that held him.

"Here, lay him in here. I've got it all ready," said Mr. Jillard, moving towards the wagon. "I thought you'd like the job I had for you, Buster."

That meeting of the brothers had been worth more to Hicks Jillard than the bag of gold he had laid by that morning He charged his memory to store away a perfect picture of it for Mrs. Jillard.

Baby Jim did not want to lie on that good soft bed. He liked best to be held firmly by the only being in the wide world who had ever loved him. It was not until he was in a sound sleep that his head was gently placed on the pillow, and he was covered up as carefully as if he were the heir apparent of a throne.

Buster had no words in which to thank Mr. Jillard for his kindness, though he

vainly tried to express the deep gratitude he felt.

"Don't say a word, boy," said the
honest farmer; "I meant it from the first,
but I didn't dare to tell you, for fear it
couldn't be. I wasn't sure he could be
moved, or there'd be any body to bring
him. The Asylum folks, however, stick
at nothing that's for the good of the
boys. God bless them."

"You'll have a blessing too, sir, that's
sure," said Buster warmly.

"I hav'n't done any thing. It was
more Mrs. Jillard. She's hankered after
that little chap ever since she heard
about him. She's an idea that her Dol-
ly's sweet milk will fetch him up, and
straighten him out; and I don't know but
she thinks his arm will grow right on
again, if she once gets the care of him.
The nights she talked about it to me,
and planned over it! Why, she's got a

mattress all fixed up for the settee in the kitchen, and she means to have him there all day, where she can look after him, she says. A'n't she a woman, now?"

"And to think she lets *me* call her mother! I wish I might be a right son to her," said Buster.

"And so you will. And so will he too. He'll serve her for a daughter in the house, where she can see him all the time and have somebody to talk to. My Mrs. Jillard likes a good listener," said Hicks, with a funny quirk of his mouth.

Buster thought of his moment of temptation the night before, the terrible struggle that had sent him trembling to his knees. Ah, if he had yielded, where now would have been the cheerful prospect that was opening before him? What sorrow and disappointment he would have brought upon the friends who had so kindly sheltered him. How sure would have been his own utter falling back into wickedness and misery.

With devout thanksgiving, Buster silently praised the God who had watched over him in his hour of peril, and brought him off conqueror, though the enemy of souls had striven to drag him down to eternal death.

CHAPTER XIII.

CONCLUSION.

SUFFERING and weakness made Baby Jim seem even smaller and younger to his brother's eyes than when they parted. Rough companions and hard usage had been his lot since then. His life had been risked as of little value, where older villains would not willingly trust their own necks. No ledge along a house was thought too narrow for him to find a footing, no trellis too slender for him to climb. He was told that if he fell, there would be nobody to cry; and if he succeeded, a golden reward was promised him, still promised him, though as yet he had barely daily bread. While Buster was at his side, even grown men would not so have treated Baby Jim. The boy

knew it, and often and longingly had his
thoughts turned towards the lost companion of his childhood. Baby Jim had
found the way of transgressors hard in ·
deed, with few rays of sunshine to cheer
the dreary path.

Now he was to be nursed and petted
as if he were some precious thing. He
had fallen among God's true children,
who count every sufferer as the peculiar
charge of Christ, to be loved and cared
for as if sent by the Crucified himself.
"Inasmuch as ye have done it unto one
of the least of these my brethren, ye
have done it unto me," were heart-
appreciated words to Mr. and Mrs. Jillard, and they rejoiced that a way was
yet left them of ministering to His neces-
sities, who while on earth had not where
to lay his sacred head.

All day long Baby Jim would lie quietly on his easy couch, taking a sort of re-

flected comfort from Mrs. Jillard's kind, cheerful face; but when the farmer and Buster came into the kitchen, he claimed a little more attention. He raised himself at once to be taken into Buster's arms, where he chiefly loved to find himself; and it was thus that he took his place at the table, where the tenderest morsels and the fairest fruit were always selected for him.

For Mr. Jillard's quizzical smile and playful greeting, Baby Jim had a quiet twinkle of the eye, that told that the farmer's fun was welcome, though it won no spoken response.

Jim gained slowly but constantly in bodily strength, though as yet he gave no sign of that true, inward progress which was most at his brother's heart. When approached on religious subjects, he was pertinaciously silent, and Buster at length despairingly said to Mr. Jillard, "I do n't believe he'll ever come right. I am all discouraged about him." Mr. Jillard's reply was prompt and plain. "You do act, Buster, as if you had to be on the ridge-pole, or else the house would blow down. You've got nothing to do with making Jim a Christian You've asked the Lord to do it, and are sure he'll hear you; but it will be in His time and way. What more do you want? Here your brother has all day long a Christian woman to watch; where will you find her equal? He sees the working of the thing. Then the Bible is read in his ears every morning, and our prayers are going up for him, where he can't help but hear them. You and I must do what we can by way of making our religion show it is the real thing in us, and that will be sure to tell. I do n't mind your now and then trying to persuade him; that is all natural and right, if you believe you are on the true track; but don't keep at him all the time. Do your duty and trust the Lord. The sun don't dart up like a shooting-star; the wheat don't make the air whiz with its fast growing. The best works go on slowly. I've great hopes for that boy. He's been brought through a great deal, and I believe there's a white robe for him and a place in the many mansions, though we can't see it yet."

Buster profited by Mr. Jillard's plain talking. He remembered the Baby Jim of old—keen and cautious, slow to come to a conclusion; but once fixed, not to be easily turned from his purpose. He could not expect, in one so differently constituted, the same religious experience he had himself passed through. He would pray, and be patient. Yet when Buster felt Baby Jim's clinging arms around him, and saw the small face looking up lovingly to his, in his heart he yearned to have his brother seek the Saviour's bosom, and look up to the eyes which "closed in death to save him." Such yearnings are in themselves of the nature of the truest prayer, the soul appealing to the present God for the choic-. est blessings for its dear ones.

Through the long winter Baby Jim was but as a tender house-plant, needing the most unwearied care and attention; but as the breath of spring touched the trees and flowers, he too seemed to revive. His eyes grew brighter, and a new strength awoke in his young frame. When Mrs. Jillard's boasted hyacinths were in blossom on the sunny side of the house, little Jim was able to get out to look at them, and as he lingered on the door-step the very pride of them all was placed in his hands. There he sat looking at the rows of full, pink-tinted blos-

soms, while Mrs. Jillard glanced from
him to the flower, her eye falling on them
both with equal satisfaction.

"I'm not pretty, like it," said Baby
Jim, expressing involuntarily his feeling
of wonder that Mrs. Jillard should gaze
so lovingly at him.

The poor bent, crippled boy, with his
pale, thin, old-looking face, was in truth
very unlike the pure sweet flower in its
perfection of beauty.

"You dear fellow, it does my heart
good to see you out in the fresh air once
more," said Mrs. Jillard, and she sat
down beside Baby Jim and put her kind
motherly arm about him.

Jim leaned against her as he whispered, "I a'n't fit to live here with you,
after where I've lived, and what I've
seen, and done myself too. I a'n't like
this," and he pointed again at the flower.

"It grew up out of the dark, dirty

ground. God made it so sweet and beautiful, and I do n't mind if it has an ugly old root all covered up in the earth. I do n't care where my Jimmy has lived. I love him, and I think God is making him one of his own dear children. Is n't it so, Jimmy? Tell your mother."

Baby Jim pressed his one hand against Mrs. Jillard's, and slowly bowed his head two or three times. She kissed him a fond loving kiss as she murmured, "Bless you, dear, God bless you."

Baby Jim rose up slowly, and moved in his unsteady way round the corner of the house. Mrs. Jillard did not follow him. He could go about safely by himself now, though he never strayed far from the kind face that had beamed so cheerily upon him through the long winter.

Mrs. Jillard's clean parlor was rarely opened. The green paper curtains shut

out the light, and within all was neatness
and darkness. At the side windows the
lilac bushes held their undisturbed reign.
They had grown until they nearly reached the roof, and in the centre of the clus-
ter of bushes was a shaded spot which
Mrs. Jillard thought only visited by the
robins who had their nests in the shrub-
bery. Other feet however found their
way to this hidden retreat, for hither
Baby Jim quietly crept. He pushed his
way through the outside undergrowth,
and then was lost from sight.

"Mother," said Buster coming quickly
up to Mrs. Jillard, who was still busy
among her flowers, "Mother, father wants
his new knife. He has broken his old
one."

"Go into the parlor and get it, my
boy; it is in the little chimney cupboard,
on the left-hand side."

Buster fumbled about in the dark

room, then stepped to the window to give himself more light. Sunshine and joy indeed burst upon him, such joy as angels know in heaven. There in his chosen retreat knelt Baby Jim, his face uplifted with the sweet, loving, tender look in it which Buster knew so well.

From the depths of his softened heart little Jim was thanking the Lord who had mercifully brought him to such a home, and praying that he might be made worthy of the loving care bestowed upon him.

Buster mechanically snatched the knife, and then quickly left the room. In another moment a strong arm was round little Jim, and the brothers knelt side by side. It was Buster's voice that spoke the deep gratitude of his soul as he drew the "lost and found" still closer to his side.

Buster could not linger, duty called

him away. Fast over the fields he was
soon speeding with a springing, joyous
step, and forth on the air sounded his
hymn of praise:

"For good is the Lord, inexpressibly good,
    And we are the work of his hand;
His mercy and truth from eternity stood,
    And shall to eternity stand."

Love, true Christian love had sought
the poor wandering wicked brothers, and
brought them to the feet of Jesus.

And can the depraved children of the
city be so reformed and made useful
members of society—of the communion
of Christ's church on earth, and of the
redeemed in heaven? The Holy Spirit
of power can wash away the darkest
stains, and purify the foulest heart.
"With God all things are possible." But
has this great and wonderful work ever
been accomplished? Go ask the benev-
olent men who labor for such institutions

as we have described, and hear their cheering reply. Yes, blessed be God, many such wanderers have been reclaimed: some are adorning earthly homes; some, we trust, are shining in heaven.

The eternal mansions are opened wide, the Master's feast is ready. To us comes the message, "Go out quickly into the streets and lanes of the city, and bring in hither the poor—that my house may be filled."